8JJs

MW00711102

THE GATHERERS

The Gatherers appear from nowhere, attacking and killing, taking away the able-bodied men, then vanishing into thin air. Whilst hunting the kidnappers, Ben Travis disappears and his partner, Wes Hardiman, vows to find him. The only clues he has are the references in a dying man's words to 'men from the sea' and 'the Island of Death'. Soon Wes hits trouble in the shape of Cabal Fisk and the lethal gunslinger called Bryce. Now it becomes a grim battle for survival against overwhelming odds.

*Books by Alan C. Porter
in the Linford Western Library:*

CORDOBA'S TREASURE
RIVERBOAT
HIGH MOUNTAIN PERIL
PIKE'S LAW
THE LEGEND LIVES ON
SHERIFF OF CROW COUNTY

ALAN C. PORTER

THE GATHERERS

Complete and Unabridged

LINFORD
Leicester

First published in Great Britain in 2002 by
Robert Hale Limited
London

First Linford Edition
published 2003
by arrangement with
Robert Hale Limited
London

British Library CIP Data

Porter, Alan C.
 The gatherers.—Large print ed.—
 Linford western library
 1. Western stories
 2. Large type books
 I. Title
 823.9'14 [F]

 ISBN 0–7089–4976–2

Published by
F. A. Thorpe (Publishing)
Anstey, Leicestershire

Set by Words & Graphics Ltd.
Anstey, Leicestershire
Printed and bound in Great Britain by
T. J. International Ltd., Padstow, Cornwall

This book is printed on acid-free paper

1

They rode out of the west on a thunder of hooves trailing a pall of dust stained red by the fiery ball of the setting sun: men with black pointed hoods over their heads and death in their hearts.

The first the wagon master leading the six wagons knew of them was his last. A bullet smashed through the front of his skull just above the left eye, blowing out the back of his head in a crimson spray laced with white bone fragments and grey gobbets of brain.

Panic swept through the small wagon train. An old man in the lead wagon managed to draw his pistol before a bullet shattered his wildly beating heart. A grey-haired woman seated next to him screamed as he slumped across her lap then she too, was silenced.

The riders knew what they were doing. In a hail of lead horses dropped in their traces bringing the wagons to a halt.

The people in the wagons were not fighters but homesteaders seeking out a promised land and soon they were rounded up in a terrified group, men, women and children. The young men were separated out, roped together and bundled into a wagon that had followed the riders in; as long, purple shadows crept across the land, the final, callous act was performed.

As the wagon with the prisoners rumbled away into the growing darkness, the hooded riders turned their guns on those left behind.

Old men, women and children fell before the brutal, withering hail of fire until all screams, cries and pleas were no more. One of the hooded men made his horse rear up and paw the air.

'Ride, Gatherers, ride!' he hollered out, and then the riders were gone, galloping in the wake of the wagon. Behind them the darkness hid the horror of the terrible massacre of the innocents.

* * *

'He's disappeared, Wes. No one's seen him. He checked in at his hotel, went out and never returned.' The worried words of Colonel Tom Paxton came back to Wes Hardiman as he stepped down from the train in Galveston.

He paused for a moment to get his bearings, letting the disembarking passengers eddy around him. The train whistle blew and the smoke stack belched black smoke clouds into the clear blue of the sky. This was where Texas ended and the blue waters of the Gulf of Mexico took over.

Galveston was an island, part of a chain of long, narrow islands separated from the mainland by a stretch of water called West Bay. From where he stood, the sea was hidden behind a line of warehouses. Gripping the handle of his carpet bag tightly, he moved off, inland, away from the hidden seafront, following in the wake of the other passengers. Soon he was swallowed up in a riot of tall, brick buildings that turned the bustling streets into small canyons.

Clad in a chestnut-brown hide jacket with matching boots and hat, blue Levis and a yellow shirt, he drew curious glances from those passing by. A little under six foot tall, dark curly hair showed beneath the hat and piercing blue eyes gazed out from a handsome, prairie-tanned face. On his right hip, hung low and tied down, the polished handle of a Colt Peacemaker jutted from a holster.

He noticed, for the most part, the men about him wore Sunday suits, round-topped derby hats and lace-up shoes and, he had to admit with a wry smile, cowboy boots were not the most comfortable to walk in.

He had been given directions to the local police station and after ten minutes found himself entering through the portals of a tall, brownstone building into an imposing reception area.

On either side, red-carpeted stairs led up to a balcony, its cream-washed walls breeched in three places by polished oak doors. Sandwiched between the stairs and below the balcony ran a long, high counter behind which sat a constable in a dark-blue uniform.

Wes was more than a little awed and had to admit that this was the poshest 'sheriff's office' he'd ever seen. All the wooden fittings were dark, polished oak. He marched up to the counter, boot heels tapping loudly on the wood-block flooring, and under the man's enquiring gaze said, 'Got me an appointment to see a Sheriff Russell, the name's Hardiman.'

The desk man consulted a book and nodded.

'March!' he bawled out, and a young man in uniform, hair slicked back, appeared at the other's side. 'Take this gentleman to see the chief, an' look lively 'bout it.' He eyed Wes. 'You are expected, sir. You can leave your bag here.'

A few minutes later, after mounting the stairs, to the balcony, he waited outside the middle one of the three doors, that bore the legend 'Sheriff Boyd Russell' on a polished, brass plaque. He barely had time to read the name before he was ushered into a spacious office full of dark-brown furniture and the door closed quietly behind him.

The walls, the lower half panelled in dark wood, the upper plastered and colour washed in soft lime, were hung with pictures. Light streamed in through a large window, spilling across a big, ornate desk. A man rose from behind the desk as Wes crossed the floor.

He was a big man in his middle forties. A mane of dark hair waved back over his head and thick, full, side whiskers cascaded down the sides of his face to his square jawline. He eyed Wes with a trace of amusement from brown eyes set deep in sockets fringed with thick, dark eyebrows. Unlike his constables, he wore a dark-brown suit, the jacket open revealing a tan vest over a light-blue shirt. He reminded Wes more of a gambler than a lawman. Only the star on his vest denoted his authority.

He held out a thick-fingered hand. 'Welcome to Galveston, Mr Hardiman,' he greeted, in a deep voice richly toned with a Texan drawl. His grip made Wes wince and left his fingers tingling. 'Take a seat.' He indicated a chair before the desk and returned to his own as Wes sat down. 'First time in Galveston, Mr Hardiman?'

'First time for me, but not for my family. Uncle on my pa's side died in the Battle of Galveston in '63. The handle's Wes, by the way. Mr Hardiman is my pa.'

Sheriff Russell smiled and leaned. back in his chair.

'A noble cause,' he replied nodding. 'I received the telegram from your

Colonel Paxton about a missing man, a Ben Travis.'

'You have some news?' Wes asked eagerly.

The sheriff pulled a wry face. 'Alas no. I have twenty constables under me and they have scoured the city, but apart from when he booked in at the hotel, he hasn't been seen since. It's sure a puzzle, Wes, unless it has something to do with why he was here? Your Colonel Paxton was not very forthcoming on that point. He said that you would explain.' He eyed Wes expectantly.

'Ain't no mystery, Sheriff. Ben an' I work together, but when this particular assignment came in I was busy, had to attend court to give evidence agin an outlaw, so Ben came on ahead. He was supposed to send a telegram each day, something the colonel insists on when a man's alone. If'n he misses, then it's taken as he's in trouble. Ben only sent the one, when he arrived, The colonel contacted the hotel and learned that

Ben had gone out that very evening an' never returned. That's when he contacted you.'

The sheriff nodded. 'I see. You mentioned an assignment?'

'Some six weeks ago a wagon train, fifty miles west of here, was attacked. The men were taken and the rest of the folks on it brutally massacred.'

'The Steadman train. Yes, I remember; tragic business. Generally believed to be the work of Mexican marauders.'

'That's the version the authorities want folks to believe.'

'Want, Mr Hardiman?' Sheriff Russell looked puzzled.

'A woman was still alive when the wagon train was found. Afore she died, she kept repeating 'the Gatherers' over and over again.'

'The Gatherers?' Sheriff Russell shrugged, 'What does it mean?'

'Four months ago, man was found floating on a log in the sea some fifteen miles off the coast. He had been badly beaten, lash marks all across his back.'

'I never heard of that,' Sheriff Russell said.

'The ship that picked him up was bound for Corpus Christi, an' that's where they took him, but he died afore they docked. He said that the Gatherers, men from the sea, had taken him and his companions. But just afore he died he said, 'the Island of Death' twice.'

'Intriguing. Are you Pinkerton men?'

Wes smiled. 'No, sir, but we do work for the government along similar lines.'

'What have you learned so far?'

'Apart from the fact that there's a whole bunch of murderous gunnies, who're calling themselves the Gatherers, riding around kidnapping menfolk — and we know of three small farming communities they've hit in the last six months 'tween here an' the Mexican border — not very much. They seem to vanish into thin air. We don't know why they are taking them, or where they are taking them to.' He shrugged helplessly and stared, puzzled, at Russell; the man was smiling. 'You find it funny, Sheriff?'

'You'll have to forgive me, Wes, it's just that you're weaving a mystery outa nothing.'

'I don't understand,' Wes said hesitantly.

'There is an 'Island of Death'; the Spanish name for it is Isla de la Muerte. It lies about fifty miles offshore. It was given that name by the sailors because o' the number o' ships wrecked on the reefs that surround it. It's a notorious place that no captain worth his salt would sail anywhere near. As to these so-called Gatherers . . .

'Galveston is not some backwater cow-town. Ships from all over the world dock here an' some are not too fussy how they get a crew.' Russell leaned back and made a steeple of his fingers before his lips. 'There has been, I'm sorry to say, an increase in press-gang activities of late. Do you know what that is, Wes?'

'I'm sure you'll be able to enlighten me, Sheriff,' Wes replied, and Russell

11

smiled thinly, leaning forward and dropping his hands to the desk top, entwining his fingers together.

'Men jump ship or die at sea. Whatever the reason, a captain suddenly finds that he is short of crew. He makes his requirements known and the press gang goes to work. They pick up drunks from the waterfront taverns, or knock a stranger over the head an' the next thing the victims know is when they wake up on board a ship miles out to sea. Then they have the choice, become a crewman or be thrown over the side.

'It's a terrible business, for these people are never seen again. Unfortunately the pressing practice is hard to stamp out. Sometimes these press gangs give themselves fanciful names and Gatherers would be a suitable name for them, and 'men from the sea' would certainly indicate sailors.' Sheriff Russell nodded. 'I might be able to offer you a suitable explanation.'

'I'm listening,' Wes replied.

'I think that the man found at sea was a double victim. He was taken by a press gang and then the ship was put on to, foundered on the Island of Death reefs. As to your missing man? If'n he was looking for the press gangs it could be that they found him first and, as no body has been found, I'm inclined to favour that as his fate an' also the fate of the wagon-train menfolk.'

'If'n you know about these press gangs why don't you step in an' stop them?' Wes wanted to know, annoyed by Russell's apparent acceptance of them.

'Because they are like the wind. They are not like outlaws riding around in a band. These men only get together when required. During the day they work at normal jobs and only word o' mouth brings them together when required. I'm sorry, Wes.'

'So am I, Sheriff. It was more than a wind that massacred defenceless women and children an' stole their menfolk. I intend to look for them and hopefully find Ben in the process.' Wes climbed to his feet. 'Thank you for your time, Sheriff.' The two shook hands and the sheriff accompanied Wes to the door.

'Keep in touch, Wes, an' I'll put some feelers out for these Gatherers. Something may turn up.'

'Much obliged, Sheriff.'

'Anything to help our country cousins,' Russell said expansively. 'But remember what I said about the waterfront, Wes: it can be a dangerous place, especially at night.'

'I'll be careful, Sheriff,' Wes promised.

'If'n you find out anything, come to me first.'

'I'll do that, Sheriff.' Wes touched the brim of his hat in a farewell gesture and headed for the stairs.

The last impression of the sheriff Wes had, after he had collected his grip from the desk, was of the man standing at the balcony rail above, watching him depart.

Wes found his hotel a short while later at the top of a narrow street that led down to the waterfront. Before entering the hotel he caught a glimpse of tall warehouses beyond which rose the masts of a ship. The hotel had obviously seen better times. The brown carpet that covered the floor of the small reception area was stained and threadbare, the ochre walls grimy, but he had known worse. His room on the second floor, overlooking the street, turned out to be surprisingly comfortable. It had been Ben's room and still contained his grip. The colonel had ordered that the room not be touched or occupied until Wes arrived.

Wes stared at his missing partner's grip and sighed heavily.

After the bustle of the crowded streets he welcomed the peace and quiet of the room. Removing the boots from his aching feet, Wes stretched out on the bed and, with hands behind head, pondered on what his next move would be.

The flickering glow of a single lamp sent shadows dancing over the rough walls. Here, there was no breeze to stir the flame, and the two men ceased their work, glancing anxiously at the lamp set on a tiny ledge in the wall to their left.

Their thin, grimy, hollow-cheeked faces shone with sweat and they looked at each other uneasily.

'We need oil for the lamp,' one man croaked, and the other nodded.

'I'll go.'

The light wavered, the yellow flame shrinking into the dark folds of the wick causing the darkness to rush in around them. The first man pushed a thin fist against his lips to stop himself from screaming, then the wick flared back into life and the darkness retreated.

The man lowered his trembling fist.

'For God's sake, be quick,' he urged hoarsely.

The other nodded and scurried away into the darkness of the tunnel, bare feet hardly making a sound on the uneven stone floor.

The other man now moved closer to the lamp, staring at the yellow flame that was gradually growing smaller and, as its size decreased, his fear grew. At the rock face beside him a thick vein of yellow sparkled in the diminishing light.

The yellow vein was pocked and gouged where the picks of the two men had bitten deep into it.

Gold!

It filled a small wooden handcart with fist-sized chunks of ore, but the fortune meant nothing to the man who was clad in dirty, tattered, white cotton pants and a grubby, torn, loosely fitting shirt. Bearded, lank hair matted and caked with dust, reached to his thin shoulders. He listened to the sounds of the tunnel.

A distant, hollow booming masked the rapid beat of his heart. He could feel its power through the soles of his bare feet; a barely perceptible shudder.

They had come too far. The thick

rock walls that held back the sea beyond had been savagely hacked into, each stroke of the pick weakening the wall. He had told them, but they would not listen. The gold was all they cared about and if he tried to argue, they responded with whips, cutting into the already lacerated flesh of his back.

He ran a rough hand across his eyes wiping away the sweat. As he did so there came an ominous, cracking sound that hit his ears with the loudness of a pistol shot, making his body jerk.

It came from the rock face and he turned, stepping back. At the same time, his eyes widened in fear. A thin trickle of water, glinting in the waning lamplight, was running down the wall from a point close to the tunnel roof.

He moved forward touched his fingers to the wetness and tasted it with a dry tongue.

Salt!

A second cracking sound, sharp and explosive, sent him recoiling back and the flame began to waver sending the shadows dancing over the walls in agitation. A foot away from the first trickle of water, a second appeared.

The man turned and began to run, heedless of the sharp stone fragments that tore at his feet, leaving bloody footprints in his wake.

He ran into the darkness towards a distant glow of light. He stumbled and fell, tearing the flesh from his knees and palms, but he felt no pain as he rose to his feet and continued.

From behind him came a dull explosive rumble. Unable to help himself he paused, peering back, and wished he hadn't, for he stared into the face of death. In the split second before the lamp went out, he caught a glimpse of a terrifying, white-foamed wall of water rushing towards him. Its predatory, growling, hissing voice filled his ears so that he could not hear himself screaming. In the darkness, the rushing water took him in its icy grip and swept him away to his death.

The first man was halfway up a

creaking, wooden ladder that climbed a vertical shaft to the next level when he heard the roaring sound from below. He began to climb faster.

The water hit the base of the ladder, ripping a section away. The flimsy lashings, holding the remaining part of the ladder to the shaft wall, parted under the weight of the man.

The luckless man screamed out in terror as, still clutching on to the ladder, he plunged down the shaft into the roaring, boiling darkness below.

2

Flynne's Tavern was on the waterfront, nestling amid the big, roomy warehouses that separated the town from the sea. It was part of a small cluster of businesses that catered mainly for the seagoing men.

Flynne's faced the sea across a broad expanse of cobbled road. Moored down at the quayside, a topsail schooner, sails furled, rose and fell gently in the calm waters.

To the west, the setting sun stained the sea a deep, bloody crimson and glittered redly on the cobbles. The long, curving waterfront seemed to stretch for miles in either direction and there were at least a dozen ships moored along its length, each attached to its own wooden pier thrusting out from the quayside on thick, wooden pilings. A half-dozen more ships were anchored out to sea.

They ranged from small, single-masted scows to huge, triple-masted, ocean-going ships, wooden-hulled and iron-hulled. Some were steamers, funnels belching black smoke, but most were sailing ships.

The frantic activity of the day had subsided, with the approach of evening, as Wes entered Flynne's Tavern. From past experience of midwestern cow-towns, the two places to pick up useful information were saloons or whore-houses. The clerk at the hotel had told him that Ben had planned to visit the waterfront on the night he had disappeared.

The batwings he was so used to pushing through had given way to glass-fronted double doors, hooked back in an open invitation to enter. Once inside though it was no different from any cow-town saloon.

Tables and chairs set out on the creaking wooden floor forced Wes take an erratic course to the long, open-ended bar that faced the door-way on the other side of the room. Lamps, hanging from wooden cross-beams, had been lit to provide a cheerful glow and send the shadows of approaching night scuttling away into dusty corners.

The place was about two-thirds full, the loud hum of conversation filling his ears as he threaded his way through the tables. A mixture of smells greeted his nose. Consisting mainly of pipe tobacco and cooking, it was the latter that reminded him that he had not eaten for some time.

Most of the clientele were either seamen or dock workers clad in dark, button-up jackets and round-necked vests. Some wore woolly hats, others a cap with a single brim, making Wes feel conspicuous in his western gear. If Ben had come this way he would have been just as conspicuous, probably more so because of his height and build and mane of silver hair.

He reached the bar and pushed his

hat back on his head as a striking-looking woman approached him from the other side of the chipped and scarred counter. She had the reddest hair he had ever seen and it fell in burnished, copper waves to her slim shoulders, attractively framing a strong, pretty face.

He estimated she could not have been more than twenty-five years old. She wore a bottle-green blouse that did little to hide her full, rounded, feminine charms before it vanished into the waistband of a grey, flowing skirt.

'Well, boyo, cowboys such as yeself are more to be found on the other side o' town. Are ye perhaps lost?' Her voice had a soft Irish lilt and amusement danced in her green eyes.

Wes returned the smile. 'No, ma'am, just hungry an' thirsty. Reckon my belly thinks my mouth's left home.'

She laughed. 'Flynne's is the place to satisfy both needs. You look like a steak and potatoes man.'

'You've got it there, ma'am,' Wes

agreed happily. 'An' I'll take a large beer to be getting on with,' he concluded, as his eyes settled on three barrels on trestles behind the bar.

'The name's Siobhan, Siobhan Flynne.'

'Of Flynne's Tavern fame?'

'The very same. I own it with my brother Sean. But he has a boat and is running cargo to Port Arthur, but he'll be back tomorrow. And you'll be . . . ?' Her eyebrows lifted.

'Wes, ma'am . . . Siobhan. Wes Hardiman.' Wes decided he liked her open, chatty approach.

'Then take a seat, Wes, and I'll be bringing your food when it's ready.'

She busied herself filling a tankard with foaming beer and Wes took it off to an empty corner table as more customers came in and clamoured for her attention. He was well into his meal when seven men filed noisily into the bar earning a raised eyebrow from Wes.

They were big men clad in western

range clothes and looking for all the world as though they had just climbed out of the saddle. They wore gunbelts and were carrying pickaxe handles in their beefy hands. They called loudly to each other and laughed harshly, but it was the seventh man, obviously the leader, who drew Wes's attention.

He was tall and fiercely handsome, clad in a black suit, white ruffle-fronted gambler's shirt and low-crowned Stetson. By the expression on Siobhan's face he and his men were not welcome at Flynne's. Already chairs were scraping back and men were falling over themselves to make a rapid exit, leaving behind half-drunk glasses and partially eaten meals.

Wes remained seated as the leader reached the bar, turned his back on Siobhan and addressed the few remaining customers.

'Good food, drink and women are to be found in Fisk's Bar,' he called out in an almost amiable tone, accompanying his words with a white-toothed smile.

As he spoke, his men moved quietly around the tavern positioning them-selves near to the remaining customers. Wes found he had a hard-faced shadow. 'I hope you are getting my point?' the leader added.

There was a second wave of chair scraping and hurried footsteps until only Wes remained.

'What do you think you're doing, Bryce?' Siobhan spoke harshly for the first time and the man turned and faced her, the smile broadening on his square-jawed features.

'The lovely Siobhan. Mr Fisk sends his regards, but not his customers. All you and your brother have to do is sell this dump to Mr Fisk and your troubles will be over.'

Siobhan's green eyes flashed. 'You've driven my customers away, Bryce, now get you and your men out of my tavern, and tell Fisk he'll have to wait until Hell freezes over before he gets his hands on Flynne's.'

He gave a mock bow. 'I'll be sure to

give Mr Fisk your answer, Miss Flynne.'

The man who had moved to cover Wes, edged a little closer, tapping the pick handle into the thick palm of his other hand.

'In case you ain't figured it out, cowboy, you bin asked to leave; now, git.' The man's voice was coarse and unfriendly.

'I ain't finished my meal yet,' Wes replied, a cold edge creeping into his voice.

The man's answer was quick and vicious. He swung the pick handle down onto Wes's plate, smashing it to pieces and scattering the remains of his meal in all directions. Gravy splattered Wes's shirt front.

'You have now,' the man hissed, resting a hand on his holstered gun.

Wes looked into the heavy, grinning, stubble-chinned face as laughter filled the air.

'Reckon I have,' he agreed quietly, dabbing his shirt front with a napkin, as he rose slowly to his feet.

The man relaxed letting the pick handle hang down. He was still grinning when, with a lightning move, Wes drew his gun and brought the barrel down hard on the top of the man's hat-crowned head. The grin remained trapped on the man's face as he sank to the floor and toppled sideways, overturning a table and chair.

Even before the man hit the floor Wes had thumbed back the hammer of his Colt Peacemaker and levelled it at Bryce. So quick and devastating had been his move that no one had time to react.

'A man sure do hate to have his meal ruined,' he said icily. 'Now, who feels hungry enough to eat a bullet?' His eyes flickered around.

Bryce gave a grudging laugh. 'That was some move, Mr . . . ?'

'Cowboy'll do,' Wes cut in, tossing the napkin aside. 'The damn fool ruined a good shirt.'

'Yes sir. I take my hat off to you, cowboy.' Bryce lifted a hand to his hat.

'If'n you don't want to eat lead, Bryce, you'd best leave the hat where it is. Known me a gambler or two who kept more'n a head in their hats.'

The smile faltered on Bryce's face. He lowered the hand to chest level and brought the other up to join it.

'Very astute o' you, cowboy. Smart; I like that in a man, but you ain't that smart. With Owens outa the way that still leaves five more, some tolerable fast draws. What do you think your chances are of walking out o' here alive?' There was a mocking tone in Bryce's voice and his full smile had returned.

Now it was Wes's turn to smile. 'No, Bryce, what do you think your chances are? If'n any one o' your men tries to pull a gun, I'll blow a hole in you. Mebbe I'll stop a bullet or two in the process, but you won't ever know 'cause you'll already be dead.'

This time Bryce's smile did fade.

'And if he missed, I won't,' Siobhan spoke up. Bryce snapped his head around to find himself covered by a

30

double-barrelled shotgun that she held unwaveringly in her hands.

He turned his gaze back to Wes, eyes expressionless, but his words were aimed at his tense men.

'Stay your hands, boys, no sense in getting shot over a plate o' steak an' potatoes,' he called out loudly. 'Our business here is finished for the night. Someone get Owens.' He turned his gaze on Siobhan as two sullen-faced men stepped forward warily and helped the now groaning Owens to his feet. 'I wonder if'n you would have used that?'

'I've got cause to,' she replied stiffly. 'You've had your fun, Bryce, now take your men and get out of here.'

Bryce smiled at her, then returned his gaze to Wes as Owens was half carried, half dragged to the door and the smile faded.

'My advice to you, cowboy, is to ride out of Galveston as quick as you can.' With that, he turned and followed his men to the door, where he paused and looked back at Wes. 'We all get lucky from time to time, but I think yours has just run out.' With those parting words he disappeared into the night.

Siobhan's hands were starting to tremble as she laid the shotgun down, smile strained as she looked across at Wes.

'You've humiliated him and hurt his pride. He'll not be forgetting that, Wes. Max Bryce is mean, almost as mean as his boss, Cabal Fisk.'

'Would you have used that shotgun?' he probed cautiously.

'Wouldn't have made much difference if I had; the gun's not loaded.'

Wes laughed and shook his head as he righted a table and chairs.

'So, who is this Cabal Fisk?'

'Someone you'd do well to keep away from.' She picked up a bottle and two glasses, as she spoke, and came out from behind the bar. 'He owns the west dock area and has a mind to own the whole waterfront.' She sat down at a table and proceeded to fill the glasses. 'Have a drink, Wes, it's on the house,' she invited, and Wes came across and dropped into a facing seat. 'Bryce works for Fisk and when Fisk tells someone to jump, Bryce and his men make sure they do it, if you get my meaning.'

'I've got a few Fisks and Bryces in my time,' Wes replied. 'How come you haven't 'jumped' yet?'

She laughed, eyes flashing. 'There are two things a man should be wary of: a mean-eyed horse and an Irish colleen, both are stubborn and unpredictable.'

'I'll drink to that,' Wes said with a chuckle.

'The more Fish tries to get Sean and me to sell this place to him, the more stubborn we become. Bryce and his men drop by every once in a while and scare the customers away, but the customers come back and it's only for one night that trade suffers.' She brushed the evening's event aside in a matter-of-fact voice.

'How 'bout getting the law involved? Seems to me you've got a pretty good case,' Wes suggested.

She threw back her head and laughed. 'The law's for the rich Texans living on the other side of town. You'll find no constable patrolling this area after dark, and precious little sight of them during the day.' She took a sip from her glass and eyed him quizzically. 'So, Wes, what brings a cowboy to the ocean? Sure and I'm thinking that there must be something going on up country for you're the second, fresh-off-the-range cowboy in the same number of weeks.'

Wes stiffened slightly in his seat. 'How do you mean?'

'A man like you turned up here just over a week ago. For sure he was bigger and broader and I had to look outside to see if he had rode in on a horse.' She giggled and cradled the glass in both hands, studying its amber contents. 'But he hadn't.' She looked back at Wes. 'Real nice fella as I recall.'

Wes felt a surge of excitement pulse through him.

'Tall, silver hair, dressed in buckskin

and answered to the name of Ben?' he asked urgently.

She focused startled eyes on him.

'Now how would you be knowing that?'

'Because he's a good friend o' mine an' seems to have disappeared.'

At his words her smile faded into a woeful expression.

'That's bad news to be sure, but it is not uncommon on the waterfront.'

'So I've heard,' Wes replied sardonically.

''Tis the press men at work, curse their souls.'

'I've heard that too,' Wes cut in grimly.

'Then you've probably heard that if your friend's body has not been found floating in the harbour then he's probably on a ship heading for Africa, or some other such faraway country.'

'Tell me, Siobhan, have you ever heard of the Gatherers?'

'Who are they, sheep-herders?' She gave a laugh and he nodded, smiling with her, but it was a smile that did not reach his eyes.

'You could say that,' he replied. 'These press men: who runs them? Say I'm a captain looking for crew an' ain't too fussy if'n the crew are willing or not, where would I go?'

'That's easy: only place to go and that's Fisk's. Cabal Fisk has a finger in many pies and some of them not too savoury. He can supply anything if the money's right, legal or otherwise, it's all the same to Fisk.'

'Sounds like the kind o' man I should meet.'

'You would be foolish to try. Fisk has an army of bodyguards under the leadership of Max Bryce. Nobody gets to see Fisk without an appointment. He spends all day in the bar, then at night he goes back to his house, a few miles west along the coast, where even more guards surround him. They have specific orders: shoot to kill any person found on his property.'

''Pears to me he's either very worried

or he has something to hide,' Wes mused.

'Probably both. He's made a lot of enemies over the years. And the way I've heard it told is that he lives in fear that someone might try and settle old scores.'

'Did Ben know 'bout Fisk's Bar?'

'I think that it came up in conversation. He asked a lot of questions. Do you think he went there?'

'It's more'n possible, if'n he thought he was on to something. Did he mention anything to you 'bout going there?'

'Not that I remember. I'm sorry, Wes.' She shrugged helplessly.

Wes downed his drink and leaned back in his chair looking thoughtful. Siobhan caught the look and shook her head.

'Don't even think of trying to get to Fisk. His guards are well trained and enjoy killing,' she said warningly. 'Your friend's gone, Wes. Take Bryce's advice and get out of Galveston. You'll be a marked man for what you did here tonight. Bryce will have already put the word out that you are not welcome and on the waterfront that means only one thing.'

'I get the picture,' Wes replied calmly.

'But do you see it? There will be no shortage of men willing to cut your throat for a few dollars.'

'I'll take my chances, ma'am,' Wes said formally. 'Ben and I go back a long way and he's laid his life on the line more than once for me. The least I can do is try and find out what happened to him.'

She shook her head sadly. 'I think you're a fool, Wes Hardiman,' she stated.

'Then mebbe you should add me to the mean-eyed horse and Irish Colleen list,' Wes returned, with a gleam of amusement in his eyes.

She eyed him solemnly then broke into an attractive laugh, shaking her head.

'I'm thinking that maybe all cowboys are crazy.' She downed her drink, refilled her glass, but Wes waved an offer of a refill aside. He wanted to keep his head clear. 'Then let me offer you two bits of advice: firstly, if you want to hang around the waterfront, dress like they do on the waterfront. At the moment you stick out like a sore thumb. Secondly, it is said that if you want to know anything that goes on around the waterfront, go and see Bosun.'

'Bosun?'

'Lives in an old cabin overlooking the sea at the end of West Street. To get there you need to keep walking until the warehouses run out and the sea starts, that's where you'll be finding Bosun's cabin. Take a bottle of rum and mention my name. If he's feeling in the mood and he likes the look of you, then maybe you'll get some answers. You may not like them, but answers you'll get.'

'Did you tell this to Ben?'

'The same as I'm telling you now,' she affirmed.

'How will I recognize this Bosun *hombre?*'

'He looks like a man who's seen everything, been everywhere and done everything, and most of it before you or I was born. You'll recognize him all right. Stay the night, Wes; there are rooms here for the weary traveller. Frustrate those who are waiting now for you to leave and would do you harm.'

The offer took him by surprise.

'Here?' He sounded as surprised as he looked.

'Sure and why not?' she challenged indignantly. 'I run a clean place and handy for anyone who wants to be near the waterfront. You can collect your things from the hotel tomorrow.'

It was a sound idea. Wes nodded. 'Looks like you've got a guest for a while.'

'I'll drink to that,' she said. 'Now will you be joining me, Wes?'

'Why not?' he replied and pushed his glass forward.

3

The man was spreadeagled in the upright frame, arms and legs pulled out sideways in an X shape, bound by thick ropes at wrist and ankle. He was a big, powerfully built man, clad only in buckskin pants. His feet were bare and the early morning sunlight shone in the mop of silver hair that framed his handsome, but battered, face. His left eye was almost closed and blood coagulated on his chin from puffy, split lips.

It had been no easy task for Ben Travis's captors to secure him in the frame. It had taken eight burly men and each showed the evidence of his struggles on their bruised and swollen faces, but eventually, outnumbered, he had lost the uneven struggle and now waited for whatever fate they had in store for him.

A man moved into his line of vision blocking the huge, vertical cliff wall of glistening black rock with its strange, stone-carved entrance over which was cut into the rock a round disc sending out spikes of flame; he had been told it represented the sun.

He shook his head in an effort to clear his vision and the fat, olive-skinned face of Ortez Cardonna, El Toro, 'The Bull', swam into view.

The man lived up to his name. He was huge. A head shorter than Ben's six foot six inches, what he lacked in height he made up for in girth. Fat he might have been, but his ample flesh — bound up in colourful Mexican garb — disguised a terrible strength. He grinned up at Ben's face from beneath the wide brim of a white sombrero, with an unpleasant smile, displaying a double row of big yellow teeth that reminded Ben of a braying mule. In his thick-fingered hands he held a vicious-looking bullwhip.

'You mus' be taught a lesson, *señor*,

that eet is no' good to cause trouble 'ere. Any other *hombre* I would have killed, but you have the beeg spirit that mus' be broken an' I, El Toro, will break you.' His eyes, almost lost in the fleshy folds of his face, glared spitefully at the bound man.

'El Marrano suits you better,' Ben spat back, and El Toro's face darkened at being called a pig. He stepped closer to Ben.

'You will die 'ere, Americano, make no mistake. An' very soon you will welcome death.' He smirked up at Ben. 'But no' before you work mucho hard.' He moved out of Ben's line of vision and around behind him. Ben tensed himself.

'Go to hell, greaser!' Ben shouted out defiantly.

His answer came in the hissing lash of the bullwhip as it cracked across his muscled back, opening up the skin in a thin, blood-oozing weal that sent an agonizing jolt of pain through his body.

He writhed in his bonds, arching his back.

'Did that hurt, *señor?* I am so sorry,' El Toro jeered.

The whip came again, and again and again until Ben's back was crisscrossed with welts and ran red with blood. Sweat ran down his agony-twisted face and fresh blood dripped from his chin where he had bit his lip. He did not realize the whipping had stopped until El Toro appeared before him smiling hugely, fat face shiny with sweat.

'Now you will work, *señor*, in the Devil's Ladle where death is the only way to escape.'

Ben lifted his head. 'Look for me over your shoulder, greaser, 'cause one day I'm gonna be there,' he grated thickly, from his blood-encrusted lips.

'*Señor*, you are dead already an' the dead can harm nobody. Get him ready an' get everyone back to work.' The last words he called out to someone Ben could not see.

From the corners of his pain-filled eyes. Ben glimpsed lines of ragged, unkempt men who had been lined up to watch his punishment, now being herded past him towards the ornate opening in the wall.

A thin bearded man, grey-matted hair reaching to his shoulders, appeared before Ben.

'Sorry, son, this is gonna hurt, but it'll stop your back from festering.' The man signalled.

Cool, welcoming water hit his burning back. For a second it soothed away the throbbing, searing pain, then it turned to agonizing fire that had Ben twisting and turning in his bonds.

'Like I said, it's gonna hurt. Salt water, but it'll clean the wounds out.'

A second cascade of water, thrown by two men with buckets from behind splashed over him and this time he cried out, unable to help himself as a second wave of searing agony set his back alight and then, mercifully, his vision dimmed and he fell, unconscious, into a painless pit of black oblivion.

* * *

Wes was a different man as he struck out along the waterfront the following morning and all thanks to Siobhan. After collecting his bags from the hotel he returned to Flynne's Tavern, pausing only briefly to send a telegram to the colonel in Tucson.

Siobhan was waiting with the promised clothes and, thirty minutes after entering as a cowboy, he emerged as a seaman.

'Not even your own mother would recognize you now, Wes,' she promised, and catching sight of himself in the hardware-store window as he passed, he could see why.

Gone were the boots and Stetson, Levis and shirt; in their place lace-up boots and dark woollen pants and a dark jacket. Under the jacket, he wore a blue and white, round-necked shirt, while on his head a squat woollen cap. A night's stubble darkened his lower face. Siobhan had nodded approvingly.

' 'Tis better you do not shave.'

He had tried to wear his gunbelt in the conventional way, but part of it had shown beneath the hem of the jacket. To conceal it, he now wore it high on his waist and, as long as he kept his jacket closed, no one would see it.

'You look the part all right, Wes,' Siobhan had said. 'But try and keep your hands hidden, they are too soft for a seaman's hands and call people shipmate.' She had kissed him lightly on the cheek as he left and the memory of her warm lips still lingered there.

The morning was bright and, though early, the waterfront thronged with people as ships took on supplies. If asked where he was from, he was a whaler from Nantucket fed up with the cold, Arctic waters and looking for a berth on a ship heading for much warmer climes.

Wes did not hurry, taking in the

sights and sounds, but it seemed no time at all that he had passed through the west docks. He had caught sight of Fisk's Bar; a large, sprawling place with an upper veranda along which the whores strutted in just their undergarments, teasing passers-by with lewd calls. Soon afterwards, Wes found the bustle of the waterfront lessening, people thinning out until only he remained, a lone figure amid a collection of old, derelict warehouses.

On either side of him, the wooden buildings rotted and crumbled as they rose drunkenly from a sea of thick, tangled weeds and grass. High up on one building was a splitting board bearing the name West Street. Underfoot, the cobbles were uneven and scattered with thick clumps of grass and weed.

He continued on until finally the buildings gave way to an area of stony earth scattered with thickets of scrub and prickly pear; beyond lay the blue waters of the Gulf of Mexico.

The ground rose forming a low bluff on the top of which squatted a single cabin of weather-seasoned timber. A narrow path led up to it and, with boots crunching on the loose stone fragments, Wes made his way towards it.

The cabin sat there with its back to the city. Wes moved around to the front where he found a railed veranda covered by a wooden overhang. In an old rocker on the veranda sat a man. If he had heard Wes's approach he made no sign, but just sat and stared out over the sea, a downward curving, cherry-wood pipe ending in a wide bowl, jutting from his mouth.

Wes moved along the front of the cabin coming to a halt before a double step leading on to the veranda, and still the man gave no indication that he was aware of Wes's presence. But at his feet a sleek black dog raised its head and stared intently, suspiciously, at Wes.

Beside the man stood a small, round, cane-topped table and beside that, coming almost up to the open cabin door, a wooden stiff-backed chair. It looked like the old man was ready for company. The open door gave no idea as to what lay within the cabin. It was just a rectangle of black. Wes turned his attention to the still figure again.

The man was old, indeed he looked incredibly old to Wes as he eyed the deeply wrinkled, weather-burnished face. He wore a shiny, peaked, sea-captain's hat with hair the colour of newly fallen snow escaping from beneath its brim.

'The sea is a harsh mistress and does not care to give up her secrets without a fight.' The old man spoke in a dry, dusty voice without taking his eyes from the sea. 'I am like that sea.' Now his head turned in Wes's direction. 'Who are you, and why are you here?' Dark eyes sunk deep into dark, bony sockets eyed him suspiciously.

'I'm looking for a man called Bosun; would you be he?' Wes called out. A distant flock of seagulls sang their

mournful songs as they glided overhead.

'Who wants to know?' Bosun spoke
up. 'But I warn ye now, if your heart be
full of blackness, intent on robbing an
old man of his few belongings then the
consequences are of your own doing, or
should I say, undoing.' Bosun broke
into a dry, cackling laugh.

Wes took a step forward, but a low
growl from behind made him turn. A
second black dog, twin to that which
lay at the old man's feet, stood a few
yards behind Wes. Its lips were pulled
back in a snarl and saliva fell in long,
silver strands from its jaws.

'No, sir, I came looking for some
answers. Wes Hardiman is my name
and Siobhan Flynne said to mention
her name.' Wes eyed the old man in
desperation, then his eyes darted back
to the dog wondering if he would have
the time to pull his gun should the
animal decide to attack. The uncom-
fortable answer was no!

'Did she mention anything else?'

There was almost a sly note in Bosun's voice.

'That a bottle of rum might ease the way some,' Wes said hopefully, the low, continuous snarl raising the hairs on the back of his neck.

The old man cackled again, removing the pipe from his lips.

'Come forward, shipmate, and join me; the dogs will not hurt you unless I deem it so.' He called out something and the snarling dog instantly settled and became silent, dropping down on to its hindquarters, gaze still fixed on Wes.

Wes moved forward on to the veranda fetching the bottle of rum from his pocket and placing it on the cane-topped table. Bosun indicated the wooden chair with a thin, fleshless claw of a hand.

'Take a seat, shipmate. Perhaps I've a mind to talk today.' He nodded as Wes sat down. The snarling dog had followed him on to the veranda, its claws clicked and tapped on the wooden boards as it turned a circle before lying down, muzzle between its front paws, eyes on Wes. 'You wear seaman's clothes yet you are not of the sea,' Bosun barked, making Wes start.

'No, sir. Siobhan thought it best that I looked the part of a seaman.' Wes removed his gaze from the dog and settled it on Bosun's seamed and lined face.

Bosun nodded. 'The fair Siobhan is a woman of wisdom,' Bosun decreed; then in a louder voice, 'Jacob, bring two glasses!'

Wes was surprised to hear movement from within the cabin, for he thought the old man was alone, and turned his head as one of the biggest, darkest men he had ever seen emerged. He had to bend almost double to get through the door and, when he straightened up his head almost touched the overhang. He made the missing Ben Travis seem small.

Wes swallowed nervously as the huge man leaned across him and placed two glasses on the table. Big, dark, unfriendly eyes stared down at Wes.

'Thank you, Jacob,' Bosun said, and when the man had returned into the cabin continued, 'Whitemen, slavers, took Jacob from his African home when he was but a lad and cut his tongue out to stop him speaking o'the deed. We met many years ago, and when I left the sea Jacob came with me. I was the only one to show him kindness and now he looks after me. As you can see, with my dogs and the good Jacob I am well protected against villains. Now what can an old sailor do for one who pretends to be a sailor?'

4

The old man listened as Wes unfolded the events that had brought him to Galveston. He held back on nothing. He was in a strange and hostile environment and felt he needed all the help he could get.

Bosun was quiet as Wes talked, peering out to the distant horizon. Afterwards, when Wes was all but talked out, the old man remained silent until he had scraped a lucifer into life and lit his pipe.

''Tis a pretty tale you tell, lad, but the answers are all there if you've a mind to see them. Fill the glasses; I've a mind for a tot.'

'I don't understand,' Wes said, as he filled the glasses with the dark spirit.

'You will, lad, you will,' Bosun said, enigmatically. He removed the pipe from his mouth and lifted the glass, holding it up to the light before taking a generous swig. Wes was more cautious and glad for it as the small sip threatened to burn the back of his throat away. He coughed and felt his eyes water.

'Jesus!' he finally managed to croak. 'What do they put in this?'

''Tis a sailor's drink, lad, and saved many a poor soul on freezing nights in the northern seas.' Amusement danced in Bosun's eyes as Wes brushed away the tears.

'Happen you're right, Bosun. Reckon a glass o' this could make a dead man sit up and sing.' Wes smiled ruefully.

'Aye, I've heard of the Gatherers. Press men on horseback who wear dark hoods, ride the night, and disappear before dawn. These men are not of the sea; they come from your world of prairie and desert. Sailors do not ride horses and carry guns to slaughter. The real press men keep to the waterfront. No, Mr Hardiman, the ones you seek will not be found on this waterfront or any other waterfront.'

'But a victim of the Gatherers said they were men from the sea,' Wes argued. 'By the way, folks call me Wes.'

'And you believed men from the sea meant sailors?' Bosun raised an eyebrow.

'What else can it mean?' Wes sounded baffled.

'You see, but you don't see. You have let others do the thinking for you and taken their thoughts as the truth.'

Wes shook his head. 'You've got me, Bosun: what am I not seeing?'

'The obvious perhaps. A dying man does not have the time left for using many words where one will suffice. Why say 'men from the sea' when sailors or seamen would have been clear enough? The deathbed is not a place to become talkative, unless he was trying to say something and men from the sea meant exactly that and not seafaring men.'

Wes eyed Bosun narrowly. 'I'm riding drag on that one, Bosun, 'cause you've lost me for sure.'

'Then the answer to a riddle may be the answer you seek.' Bosun was clearly enjoying himself now. 'When is a man from the sea not a sailor? The answer is simple, lad: when he is a passenger. Does that make it any clearer? If you came to Galveston by boat then would it not be true to call you a man from the sea and not a sailor?'

Wes's eyes lost their dazed, helpless look as Bosun's words sank in. He frowned as thoughts flipped through his mind and animated his eyes with excitement.

'I lost the trail back there a ways, Bosun, but I think I'm back on it now.' He looked at Bosun. 'What you are saying is that the Gatherers come by boat to do their dirty work? It figures. They take men prisoners and then vanish into thin air, but the only place they've gone is back to their boat. So while everyone searches on land they are safe at sea.'

'That's it, lad, you're beginning to see for yourself,' Bosun applauded.

'But why? Where do they go? What happens to their prisoners? The horses the Gatherers ride, where do they keep them, or do they travel on the boat with them?' Wes shook his head in vexation. So many unanswered questions.

''Tis a ticklish problem,' Bosun agreed, lighting his pipe again and sending clouds of acrid smoke coiling upwards. 'But there are possibilities. Did you know that Cabal Fisk was once a common seaman? It was never clear how he suddenly came into wealth great enough to afford to buy the bar, the land he owns further along the coast, and the house he had built on it — a rather splendid mansion.'

'That could answer a couple o' questions,' Wes admitted.

'Rather more than you think, lad. Cabal Fisk also owns two boats, one that he keeps moored in a private cove that is part of his land.'

'Just give me the reason why an' I'll be a happy man.'

'Maybe your missing friend found

the answer and that's the reason he's missing, for he never came here.'

'That would be just like Ben,' Wes agreed. 'Do you know Fisk well, Bosun?'

'We shipped out a few times together. He captained a small brig, a coastal trader, but we did not see eye to eye, so to speak, so it was a short acquaintance. It was during that time that I met Jacob. Fisk's treatment of him was less than human so when I changed ships I took Jacob with me.'

'I take it that there was no love lost between you an' Fisk?' Wes said shrewdly.

'You could say that, but it was a short time after that that Fisk's boat, the *Sea Angel*, came to grief on the reefs around Isla de la Muerte and for his crew it was the Island of Death. It was two months later that a fishing boat, attracted by smoke from the island, found Fisk still alive and managed to rescue him. It was not long after that that Fisk suddenly became a man of wealth. He said it was money inherited from a rich uncle on his father's side.' Bosun shrugged.

'You don't believe that?' Wes prompted.

'I can neither prove nor disprove it, lad. Strange things happen at sea,' Bosun concluded. 'Are you going to drink that rum?'

Wes laughed ruefully. 'It's a bit too strong for my taste, Bosun.'

'Then pass it across, it's too good to be wasted.'

They talked for a while more and then Wes said his goodbyes promising that he would let Bosun know if he found out anything more. As he walked back to the waterfront, he let his mind toy with what Bosun had told him.

There was no hard evidence against Fisk to say that he had anything to do with the Gatherers, but it was all he had to go on and that was a start. So intent was he on turning the problem over in his head that he let his mind relax to the possible dangers inherent in his isolated surroundings.

Movement on the edge of his vision brought him to a halt. Two dark-clad figures had emerged from between the crumbling, rat-infested buildings that lined West Street; grimy, sullen-faced individuals flanking him on either side. Moving with him, stopping now that he had stopped.

'Good day, shipmate. You must be lost to be on this part of the waterfront.' A third man stood blocking his way, giving him a gap-toothed smile from a battered, weathered face, his voice throaty and rasping. He was bigger than the other two, dark strands of lank hair issuing from beneath a cap.

'No, I reckon I know where I'm going,' Wes replied.

'Maybe you're in for a surprise, shipmate,' the man intoned nastily.

'Maybe you are, too,' Wes snapped back, as two more men appeared from between the buildings on either side and joined the speaker. One wore a battered derby, the other . . . Wes stared in fascination.

'Mr Collins and Mr Weems,' the speaker introduced, 'and I be Crow. By the way, the other two gents be Scratch and Mole. Now, who might you be?'

'Your worst nightmare if'n you don't step aside,' Wes replied calmly, dragging his gaze from the one called Mr Weems, for the man was wearing a tan Stetson that Wes recognized instantly as belonging to Ben. He settled his gaze on Crow. Crow's eyes widened.

'That don't sound too friendly, shipmate.'

'It wasn't meant to be.' Wes was aware that Scratch and Mole were slowly edging their way towards him. Out of the corner of one eye he caught a flash of silver in Mole's hand, and his heart quickened as adrenalin pumped through his veins.

Ahead of him the men either side of Crow had produced short cudgels from their coats while Crow had opened his coat over a ponderous belly to reveal a gunbelt that Wes had no difficulty in recognizing as Ben's with handle of the British-made Adam's protruding from the holster.

'Well, lads, 'tis time we taught our shipmate the proper respect he should show his betters,' Crow smirked. 'Look lively, lads, by the cut of his jib his pockets should be full of a sailor's pay and we know how to spend it.'

Scratch and Mole quickened their pace as Weems and Collins started forward, leaving Crow, hands folded across his chest, to watch.

Anger surged through Wes joining with the frustrations of the past few days. Scratch, a thin man his face covered in pox scars, was a step or two ahead of his companion Mole and became Wes's first target.

Standing his ground, Wes took his weight on his right leg, raised his left leg and drove his booted foot hard into the man's knee. There was an ominous crack. Scratch gave an anguished scream and fell to the ground, writhing in agony, hands clasping his shattered knee. As he went down, Wes opened his coat and pulled his gun.

He spun to face Mole, lashing out with the gun, whipping the hard barrel of the Colt Peacemaker across Mole's prominent Adam's apple before bringing it down with savage force on the top of his skull. The man dropped heavily to the cobbled roadway and lay still.

The efficient despatching of the two men took only seconds. Weems and Collins had covered hardly any ground before they found themselves covered by Wes's gun and came to a confused halt.

Weems threw his cudgel down and clawed at the sky with his hands. Collins, the stockier of the two, held on to his and treated Wes to a sullen glare. Crow was desperately trying to draw the Adam's, but it had snagged on his clothing.

'Don't try it, Crow. It takes a good man to use that gun an' you ain't he,' Wes called out.

Crow snatched his hands away from the gun and held them out before him.

'Don't be too hasty, shipmate. We can, ah, talk about this little misunderstanding.' Sweat had broken out on his face.

'Don't worry, mister, we are gonna talk. Unbuckle the gunbelt an' let it drop or I'll take if off your dead body.'

'You can have it!' Crow replied, quickly and with trembling hands unbuckling the gunbelt and letting it drop.

'Mr Collins, that hand you've put into your pocket had better come out empty,' Wes called out sharply, the derby-wearing man's stealthy movements not lost on Wes while he had been addressing Crow.

Collins froze, sullen eyes on Wes.

'How 'bout I put a bullet in your fat boss if'n you don't bring that hand out clean?' Wes said.

'For Gawd's sake, Collins, do as he says,' Crow hissed in alarm.

Slowly, silently, Collins began drawing out his hand, but at the last minute pulled it free in a blur of movement to reveal the small, Remington-Eliot, four-barrelled pocket pistol popularly known as the 'Pepperbox'. His finger was tightening on the trigger when Wes's Peacemaker spoke. The heavy bullet blew a hole in Collins's chest and sent the man staggering back, his eyes popping wide in surprise, blood exploding from his mouth and flooding down his chin.

The look of surprise was still on his face as his legs collapsed beneath him and he fell face down on the cobbles, the Pepperbox pistol flying from his grasp and skidding across the cobbles to end up at Wes's feet.

'There's allus some fool who wants to try it the hard way,' Wes murmured. He stepped closer to the remaining two men, thumbing the hammer back in a series of dry clicks before placing the mouth of the Peacemaker against Crow's sweating forehead. 'You're both wearing something that belongs to a very good friend o' mine; a gun an' a hat. Now, as he wouldn't part with either willingly, how come you have them, an' I don't mind who answers?'

'We found 'em,' Crow shrilled and Weems nodded.

Wes shook his head sadly. 'Ain't good enough, Crow. Mebbe when Weems here sees you get a bullet in the brain, he'll be more apt to say what I want to hear. Goodbye, Crow.'

Crow's eyes fastened on Wes's tightening finger and his face became white and haggard.

'No, please, please,' he begged. 'I'll tell you, I'll tell you!' He sank to his knees clasping his hands together before him as though in prayer.

5

It took less than ten minutes for the whole sordid story to come out. Crow and his men had been hired by Bryce to waylay Ben, who had been in Fisk's Bar asking questions about the Gatherers. Bryce did not want Ben killed, so Crow and his men had jumped the big cowboy, beaten him unconscious and delivered him back to Bryce bound hand and foot. That was how they had acquired the gunbelt and hat.

'He was alive when we handed him over,' Crow said, and Weems backed him up.

'They was waiting for us,' Weems took up the story. 'Put him in a wagon and drove off.'

'And the direction they took only leads to Fisk's house,' Crow added. 'Now please, shipmate.'

Wes stepped back and holstered the

gun. Behind him, Scratch was still moaning and holding his broken knee and Mole was beginning to come to. Nobody had appeared to investigate the gunshot. People on the waterfront tended to keep themselves to themselves.

Wes retrieved Ben's gunbelt and hat, picked up the Pepperbox pistol and tossed it into a thick clump of weeds.

'Well, thank you, boys, you've been real helpful; mind you, I don't think Bryce is gonna see it that way when he finds out, but don't let that spoil your day.'

* * *

'You killed a man you say?' Sheriff Russell eyed Wes sternly across the desk as later that day Wes gave him the full story of events. 'That's a serious matter. We don't take too kindly to your inland methods of dealing with trouble.' He gave Wes a glare to indicate his displeasure.

The sheriff's manner irked Wes some. Normally good at keeping his feelings under control, frustration and worry over the past few days pushed tact and diplomacy aside.

'I don't give a damn what you take to, Sheriff. A good friend o' mine is missing; men are being taken by force, an' their loved ones butchered on the trail by a pack o' gunnies in masks. You have a waterfront that is a law unto itself and the man I consider to be at the heart o' it remains free. As to the man I shot? If'n I hadn't shot then I wouldn't be here now for he, sure as hell, woulda plugged me. I've given you the evidence; pull Crow and his men in for questioning.'

'Evidence!' Russell, his face reddened by Wes's onslaught, raised his voice, leaning forward on his desk. 'The word of a crazy old man living alone who never leaves his cabin; a group of waterfront thugs terrorized by you into telling you what you want to hear. I hardly call that evidence, and as to

Cabal Fisk,' — Russell paused to gather breath — 'he may run a rowdy bar, but that is the nature of his clientele.

'Men who spend months at sea come ashore looking for a place to let off steam. If it wasn't for Fisk's Bar these men would venture further into town causing havoc and making more work for my constables. No, Mr Hardiman, Fisk's Bar keeps the rough element contained and that I welcome. What I don't welcome is an outsider stirring up trouble and I shall make that known to your Colonel Paxton.'

'You do that, Sheriff, an' I'll do what I came here to do, with or without your help,' Wes said bluntly, blue eyes flashing.

'I would advise you to step carefully around Cabal Fisk. He is a powerful man in Galveston and has some equally powerful friends, the Governor of the State of Texas being one of them. Step too far out of line and it could be that you'll end up behind bars. Do I make myself clear?'

'Perfectly,' Wes said drily climbing to his feet. 'But then I'm just a poor country boy.'

Russell sighed and leaned back in his chair.

'Wes, I can understand how you feel 'bout the loss of your friend and I'll allow that on this occasion it has coloured your judgement somewhat.' Russell's tone had dropped into something near sympathy. 'The waterfront is a complex world of its own. They stand together if trouble threatens and deal with it in their own way. If you cause trouble there I can't help you.'

'*Won't*, it seems to me,' Wes replied acidly.

This time Sheriff Russell would not be drawn. He shook his head.

'I'll try and explain it to you. Cabal Fisk runs the waterfront and we have an unwritten agreement that neither of us encroaches on the other's territory. It may not seem lawful to you, but it's a system that works to everyone's satisfaction. The streets of the town are not filled with drunken sailors causing trouble and the waterfront is not patrolled by constables. It may not be a perfect system or strictly legal, but it maintains the delicate balance between the waterfront and the town.'

'Which lets Fisk do what he wants like sending the Gatherers out on man-hunting raids,' Wes sneered.

'On the contrary. Fisk knows that he is not above the law and were it proved that he was connected with any criminal activity then I would personally see to it that he was convicted. So unless you can produce some hard and real evidence to link Fisk with the Gatherers, then I would keep your suspicions to yourself.'

'Oh, don't you worry, Sheriff, I'll find the evidence all right,' Wes snapped, 'and when I do I will expect your full co-operation in arresting him.'

'You have my assurance on it,' Russell promised.

'Then I'll be in touch,' Wes said, and

marched out of the office without a
backward glance.

★   ★   ★

'Sure and the sheriff will not touch
Cabal Fisk,' Siobhan said scornfully
after Wes had returned to the inn and
relayed his meeting with Russell to her
and a newcomer. The newcomer, a tall,
well-made man with a shock of red hair
and smiling face took up the story.

'And haven't we been to the sheriff
before, those of us who are honest
traders, and complained of the 'moor-
ing fees' Fisk takes off us for the use of
the waterfront? He said it was nothing
to do with him.' The face of the
newcomer, Sean Flynne, Siobhan's
brother, darkened. 'If we don't pay then
something happens to our boats.' He
slapped a hand noisily down on the
table top that the three sat around in
Flynne's Tavern. 'He even has the run
to Corpus Christi for his boats only,
leaving the rest of us to fight over the

75

run to Port Arthur.'

'I wonder why,' Wes mused.

'What are you thinking, Wes?' Siobhan asked, eyes searching his face carefully.

'I don't know yet. It's just that all the raids the Gatherers make take place between here and Corpus Christi. Mebbe Fisk has a reason to keep other eyes away. Bosun said he had two boats.'

'*The Hawk*, a two-masted brig and *The Raven*, a fast, three-masted sloop,' Sean answered.

'Might be interesting to find out when the boats were last in Corpus Christi. See if'n there was any unusual delays in leaving here and reaching Corpus Christi. I'm reckoning on the captured men being taken away by sea, but where do they take them?'

'If I was a gambling man, I'd bet my last dollar that they are being taken out to sea and transferred to a seafaring ship that is short of crew,' Sean replied emphatically, and Siobhan nodded her head in agreement.

'Sean's right, Wes; that's why they are never seen again. Probably crewing a ship to Africa or the Indian ocean.'

'I ain't saying you're wrong, Sean, but I'm still gonna check up on Fisk's boats,' Wes said rising to his feet. 'I'll get me a telegram off to my boss. The colonel is a wily ol' bird an' no doubt knows someone in Corpus Christi who can supply the information.'

* ★ ★

The Devil's Ladle was like something out of a nightmare, but ten times worse because it was no nightmare from which a person could awaken: it was awful reality.

The long handle of the ladle was a circular shaft that dropped down into the bowels of the earth, to merge with a lofty cavern a hundred feet below. The cavern spread away from the shaft to form the bowl of the ladle.

It was perhaps thirty feet wide and

twice that in length. Kerosene lamps, set in niches along the rough, dark walls, formed isolated pockets of lambent, yellow light that heightened the gloom rather than decreased it, never quite penetrating the darkness that hid the cavern roof twenty or thirty feet above.

The biggest concentration of light came from a huge, treble-tiered scaffold formed from wooden piles and rough planks lashed together with ropes. This rickety structure festooned the far end of the cavern like some monstrous, ungainly spider web.

It was hung with a dozen or more lamps, their combined light just enough to illuminate the clustered, tapered columns of stalactites hanging from the roof above the scaffold.

Ben had been lowered down the shaft by means of a square, wooden platform, its four corner ropes forming a pyramid overhead, the apex of which was attached to a single, creaking cable coming from a hand-operated winch.

Accompanied by two guards, he had been unceremoniously thrown out at the bottom and the platform raised.

Painfully, the lash marks on his back seeping blood, he climbed to his feet, using an arm to steady himself against one of four stout, wooden props. These formed a receiving cage for the platform to slide into on its final descent into the cavern. The cavern was filled with a dulled, muted boom like distant, continuous thunder.

Figures moved in the pockets of light and Ben stared in growing horror as they shuffled forward silently; gaunt, haggard figures in ragged clothing that hung like dirty shrouds from their thin, half-starved bodies. Straggly beards hung in matted tangles from their chins while lank hair embraced their heads falling to their bony shoulders. In their eyes Ben saw the look of men who had lost all hope; men waiting for the welcome embrace of death to release them from the endless horror of the Devil's Ladle.

The sight of them made the big man forget his own aches and pain. He pushed away from the prop.

'My name's Ben,' he called out, his voice ringing hollowly in the confines of the cavern, its loudness causing those nearest him to cringe back. Then, one by one, the hapless creatures, there were seven in all, turned away from him and shuffled back into the gloom and shadow.

'They don't say much, shipmate. Fact is, they don't say anything.' An eighth figure moved into the light. He was of medium height and stockily built and in a better condition physically than the others, but his once broad face was beginning to hollow as the cheeks sank. Bearded, he had somehow managed to cut the beard back. 'Jonas Flagg is me name, and glad I am to have someone to talk to.'

'Good to meet you, Jonas.' Ben frowned. 'What's the noise?'

'That be the waters of the Gulf of Mexico banging at the door to be let in.

One day they will come flooding in and all our troubles will be over.' He sounded almost joyous at the thought.

'Are there no guards down here?' Ben looked around.

'Guards, Ben? This is the Devil's Ladle and guards ain't needed 'cause there ain't no way out accept by winch.' Amusement danced in Jonas's eyes as he surveyed Ben. 'We're put down here to dig gold and die, an' that's the horrible truth of it.'

'Why dig the gold if'n you know you'll never get out?' Ben asked.

'The reason is simple enough: no gold, no food. They send the platform down once a day to collect the day's diggings. If it's enough they send it down again with food and water, if you can call the slop they give us food. Funny thing the will to survive, Ben. Even down here where hope is gone altogether, no one's willing to starve themselves to death. We all work in the hope that a miracle will occur.'

'An' just where about are we exactly?

Texas, Mexico?'

'Neither, shipmate, we're on an island called the Isla de la Muerte, the island of Death, fifty miles out to sea from Galveston and it might as well be a thousand for all the good the knowing of it is. Ships give this place a wide berth on account of the reefs that surround it. Many a ship's foundered in these waters so none comes near now.'

Ben digested that piece of unwelcome information silently.

'How long you been here, Jonas?'

'Don't rightly know, but I was here before most of these.'

'How come you don't look like them?' Ben asked bluntly, a sudden suspicious look flaring in his eyes that was not lost on Jonas.

'Calm yourself, shipmate Ben. I'm an old seadog. Spent a lifetime at sea. Faced death more than once and that tends to make a man a survivor. These poor souls are landlubbers, taken by the Gatherers and brought here to work in the mines. Now they don't know how to survive. How about you, Ben, what ship are you from?'

'The same 'ship' as them,' Ben replied grimly. 'Been trying to find these here Gatherers, but reckon they found me first.'

'Trouble is you'll never be able to tell anyone now.'

'I don't intend staying in this hell-hole. Gotta good friend who'll be looking for me now.'

'He'll have to be smart to find this place,' Jonas sang out.

'He's better'n smart,' Ben replied with conviction. But in his mind the shadow of a doubt appeared.

★ ★ ★

It was two days later that Wes returned to Flynne's after a visit to the telegraph office and slumped into a chair at a corner table frowning deeply. Sean, who had been helping his sister at the bar, came across.

'You look troubled, Wes.'

'Puzzled would be a better word,' he said, pulling a square of paper from his pocket as Sean sat down. 'You remember I sent a wire to find out 'bout the movements of Fisk's ships.'

'And?' Sean prompted.

'Seems that *The Raven* pays a regular visit to Corpus Christi, but *The Hawk*? There's no record of it docking at any port between here and Corpus Christi.'

Sean raised an eyebrow.

'But that's impossible. I've seen it at sea many a time heading on a western tack.'

'So where does it go then?'

6

'That's not possible, someone's made a mistake,' Sean said vigorously. '*The Hawk* sets sail on the evening tide each Tuesday and Friday and is back in berth the following evening.'

'How long does it take to reach Corpus Christi by sea?' Wes asked.

'Depends on the weather and the ship,' Sean said with a shrug. 'Two, maybe three days.'

'But *The Hawk* is back here in two days, so where does she go? What's out there that she can get to and back again in that short time?'

'Maybe she only goes to Freeport. That she could do easily in the time available.'

Wes consulted the square of paper that contained the telegram from the colonel.

'Corpus Christi, Port Lavaca and

Freeport. The harbour masters all say the ship never docked at their ports.' He tossed the telegram to Sean who read it, shaking his head negatively, before passing it back.

Sean passed a hand wearily across his eyes and shook his head.

'I don't understand, Wes. Let me make some enquiries.'

'Be careful, Sean. Fisk has a lot of ears out there working for him,' Wes warned.

The big Irishman grinned. 'Now don't you be worrying yourself, Wes. I know which skippers I can trust. I'll see you back here later. What will you be doing?'

'Mebbe go an' see Bosun again.'

'Well, see that you take care after what happened the last time.'

It turned out to have been a non-eventful time for both men when they met again that evening.

'Your information is correct, Wes. *The Hawk* has not been seen at any port, east or west of Galveston,' Sean said without preamble, as he dropped dejectedly into a chair opposite Wes in Flynne's Bar. The early evening sun hit the windows at an angle sending bars of red and gold slanting across floor and tables. The few customers that were in the bar occupied half-a-dozen tables. All had what they wanted for the moment so Siobhan joined the two.

'Could it be that she meets another ship out to sea?' She posed the question after listening to the day's events.

'Anything's possible,' Sean agreed.

'What about the island?' Wes spoke up.

'Isla de la Muerte? That's the one place ships keep away from. 'Tis the graveyard of many fine vessels.'

'But the island can be reached?' Wes persisted.

'By a shallow-hulled ship that doesn't draw too much water,' Sean agreed and his eyes narrowed. 'Why the interest in the island? There's nothing there.'

'Mebbe, mebbe not,' Wes said enigmatically. 'Is *The Hawk* shallow-hulled?'

'She is.' Sean eyed Wes keenly. 'What have you heard that makes you ask about the island?'

'Just something that Bosun said the other day, 'bout Fisk being shipwrecked on that island one time and how he was the only survivor. It just strikes me as odd that out of a full crew, and Bosun said today that it would have been over fifty men, only Fisk should survive. Doesn't that seem a mite odd to you?'

'What exactly are you getting at, Wes?'

'Just say I've got a suspicious mind and humour me.'

Sean and Siobhan eyed each other and then Sean shrugged at Wes.

'I guess it's odd,' he agreed slowly. 'I would have expected more survivors. Are you trying to say that Fisk' — Sean lowered his voice and leaned towards Wes — 'killed any other survivors?' Sean sat back shaking his head. 'That doesn't make sense, Wes. What possible reason could he have had for doing such a thing?'

'I'll have to agree with Sean on this, Wes,' Siobhan cut in.

'Only one way to find out,' Wes said, 'an' that's to go and have a look.'

Before either Sean or Siobhan could frame a suitable reply, a man burst through the front door and into the bar.

'There's smoke rising from the west dock area. Looks like old Bosun's place,' he called out excitedly, and then charged back outside.

There was a noisy mass exodus from the bar as every man wanted to see. Outside, people had stopped, craning their heads in the direction of the setting sun that was partially obscured by oily swirls of thick, black smoke rising into the sky above the far warehouses.

A wagon and pair, its driver just finished delivering supplies to a ship, stood across the way. Sean grabbed Wes's arm and steered him towards it. Sean knew the driver and after a few quick words the man nodded. Sean turned to Wes.

'He'll take us there. Climb aboard.'

Five minutes later, after a bone-jarring trot that had set people scattering on either side, the driver pulled the wagon to a halt at the far end of West Street and the two jumped down. Quite a few people had arrived already and stood in a silent, ragged semi-circle viewing the cabin that was now well alight, engulfed in a roaring, hissing ball of yellow flame.

Wes pushed through a knot of people with Sean on his tail and cast around for a sight of Bosun or the huge Jacob, but none was forthcoming and he felt a hand tighten around his heart.

'Did Bosun get out?' Wes called to one of the spectators, and the man shook his head negatively.

Wes looked back at the furiously burning cabin with a sinking feeling as the roof collapsed sending whirling spirals of sparks to join the dark clouds of ascending smoke.

He felt the heat from the flames roll over him then something caught his eye a few yards ahead, partially hidden in a rocky hollow. He moved forward. It was one of Bosun's dogs. It had been shot. He cast around as the fire crackled in his ears and it was not long before he sighted the other dog. It too had been shot.

Sean moved to Wes's side as the latter rose to his feet from examining the second dog.

'No one seems to know how it started,' Sean said.

'I'm thinking it's no accident,' Wes said grimly, indicating the dead animal. 'It's been shot and so has the other one!' He jerked a thumb in the direction of the first dog.

'The devil you say,' Sean returned, then he caught hold of Wes's arm and pointed out to sea through the drifting smoke. 'There, Wes, *The Hawk*!'

Wes followed the direction of Sean's pointing finger and saw the tiny, dark shape of the schooner beating a south-westerly course away from Galveston. He watched for a few minutes then turned away.

'Let's get out of here,' he said abruptly, and a cold, hostile gleam shone in his eyes. 'I think it's 'bout time Cabal Fisk an' I got acquainted.'

* * *

Ben watched the platform ascend the shaft away from him carrying its cargo of gold ore to the upper level and freedom.

'Don't even think about it, Ben,' Jonas warned from behind.

'Think 'bout what?'

'The possibility of perhaps hanging from the bottom and getting a free ride to the top.'

Ben turned and scowled down at the grimy, shadow-etched face of Jonas. Beyond Jonas, across the shadow-haunted floor of the cavern, on the crude scaffolding, men continued working at the rock face. The metallic ring of iron picks on stone rang through the cavern joining with the hollow drum of the sea into a mournful dirge.

'Now how'd you know what I was thinking?' Ben demanded.

'Because we've all had the same idea at one time or another. Knowed one shipmate who tried, but them fellas topside, they were ready. They always raise the platform high before settling it in position, so's they can see underneath it.'

'What happened?'

'Well he figured that if they caught him he'd just get a beating and be sent back down again. He was right about the coming down again, but not in the way he thought.' Jonas gave a grim chuckle. 'He figured it was worth the effort only they wouldn't let him up. Made him stay there, clinging to the bottom o' the platform, until he could no longer hold on. Nigh on a hundred feet from top to bottom. Broke nearly every bone in his body except his neck, which would have been kinder. Took him three days to die.'

Ben felt a cold shiver run over him.

'They don't hold life as precious here then?'

'Cheapest commodity of all is life, shipmate Ben. When they run low they just send the Gatherers out to get some more.' Jonas chuckled softly to himself.

'You sure are a comfort in time of stress,' Ben said sarcastically.

'The sea does that to a man,' Jonas replied. 'I'll tell you another of their little surprises. Old Billy Wragg thought he could outsmart them. You see, when a body dies we just holler up the shaft that a corpse is coming up with the next load. Well, Billy thought he'd play dead in the hope o' taking them by surprise, only it was he who got the surprise.' Jonas paused, shaking his head.

'So what happened?'

'The guards are real cautious. Just to make sure a dead body is dead they shoot it full o' holes. Poor old Billy sure was dead after that.' Jonas broke into another chuckle.

Ben eyed him distastefully. 'Got any more bedtime stories?'

'There's the dogs.'

'Dogs?'

'Raised in hell I shouldn't wonder, an' definitely not man's best friend.' This time he shuddered. 'Workers in other parts o' the mine are not as,' — he gave a sardonic smile — 'how shall we say, 'fortunate' as us? They can an' do escape from time to time.'

'How come that makes us fortunate an' them not?'

'Because they set them infernal dogs loose. Even the guards lock themselves away when them brutes are out for they'll attack anything or anyone that moves. Only their handlers can control them. Four dogs, four handlers. Ain't nowhere to run on this accursed island, shipmate, an' nowhere to hide from them hounds o' hell. They've been trained for one thing an that is to kill an' they do it well. Seen a man throw his'sel off the cliff onto the rocks below rather than face them dogs.'

'For a prisoner, you sure know a lot of what goes on around here.'

'So I should, shipmate; I used to be part o' it once; a guard.'

Surprise filled Ben's eyes at the revelation.

'How come you're down here now?'

'Thought I could get away with some of Fisk's gold. Cabal Fisk, he runs this hell hole. I was stashing a little bit away each time a load came up, had it all planned. Next short leave, I was going to have it away and live the life of a rich man. Trouble was they found it and I ended up down here. Greed is man's downfall.' Jonas shook his head sadly.

'It will be when I get my hands on this Fisk character,' Ben promised darkly, the reflected light of the lamps giving his eyes an unholy gleam.

Jonas looked up at him. 'You have amazing optimism for a man with no future,' he said admiringly.

'Could say the same 'bout you,' Ben cut back.

*   *   *

'What do you hope to gain by it, man?' Sean had argued.

'Personal satisfaction. Seems that this Cabal Fisk holds all the cards around here. 'Bout time I played a few o' mine.'

Wes remembered his last words with Sean as he entered Fisk's Bar and pushed his way through the crowd, eyes watering in the haze of tobacco smoke that filled the big room with a grey, choking fog.

The noise was intense. A piano rattled away in one corner while on a small stage a blowsy woman in a red dress sang a song. She had an audience of perhaps a dozen men admiring more the way her ample bust heaved in the low-cut dress than the contralto notes issuing from her painted lips.

Wes had changed out of the seaman's garb and was back in his comfortable, familiar range clothes and Stetson. There was a smattering of cowboy hats amid the sea of dark caps and no one paid any attention to him as he meandered a crooked path between the many tables. He was heading for a closed door beneath a set of wooden stairs across to the left. The stairs climbed to a balcony where a set of six doors opened and closed with monotonous regularity as men made drunken visits to the bar whores.

Below the balcony ran a long bar behind which ten barkeepers worked feverishly to keep thirsty customers supplied with drink. They were lined up three deep at the bar and the singer's voice became lost in the constant hoarse bellow of men demanding to be served.

As Wes pushed through a group of men, a slim figure appeared from nowhere and flung her arms about his neck.

'Hi, honey, you wanna buy a lady a drink an' have a good time?'

Wes found himself looking down into a pair of smoky-blue eyes in a pretty face, but the face came out of a jar. Heavy make-up filled the creases and smoothed the lines and the breasts pressed hard against his chest showed the bruising marks that thick, calloused fingers had left behind. Wes guessed that she was in her early twenties, but without the make-up would have looked a good ten years older.

He detached the arms gently from around his neck.

'Got me some business to do first, darling, but after that you can have as many drinks as you like,' he promised, smiling.

'Hey, Maisie. Get over here, girl!' a voice hollered from the right.

'I look forward to that,' she cooed. 'Gotta go now.' She turned away and headed in the direction of the voice.

Wes could still smell her cheap perfume as he reached the alcove under the stairs. Here a man sat at a table before the closed door, a big, sausage-fingered man with heavy, flabby jowls set in a ferocious face beneath black hair, slicked back and pomaded in places. Behind the closed door, Cabal

Fisk and a select few played poker.

'When Fisk is there the door is always guarded,' Sean had told him. Wes smiled thinly to himself. Tonight Fisk was here.

The guard looked up as Wes's shadow fell across him.

'What do you want?' the man asked sullenly, the fingers of his right hand closing around the shaft of a thick, homemade club that lay on the table.

'I've come to see Mr Fisk,' Wes said brightly.

'You gotta have a . . . ' — the man searched for the word he needed, face contorting through a series of expressions, finally ending in one that Wes took for triumph — ''pointment.' He glared at Wes from beneath a furrowed brow. 'You got a 'pointment?'

Wes did not appear to move, or so the man would swear later, but suddenly there was a gun in Wes's hand, the end of the barrel pressing hard against the guard's forehead, between his popping eyes. Sweat appeared on the man's fleshy features as Wes thumbed back the hammer grinning sardonically.

'This is the only "pointment" I need,' Wes said softly, eyes hard and icy. 'Do you have a problem with that?'

The guard shook his head as much as he dared with the gun barrel pressed against his forehead.

Cabal Fisk looked up irritably as the door opened and the guard appeared.

'What is it, Meaker?'

The unfortunate Meaker gave a startled cry as something hard and unfriendly slammed into the back of his head. As he began to sag at the knees a booted foot placed in the small of his back propelled him forward into the room and sent him sprawling to the floor where he lay without moving.

The five men at the table came abruptly to their feet, chairs overturning as Wes stepped into the room and closed the door behind him.

'Easy, gents,' he warned, eyes flickering around and settling for an instant on Bryce. 'Don't even think 'bout it, Bryce, or it's likely to be your last thought.'

Bryce smiled coldly and lifted his hands shoulder high, palms facing outward. Keeping his eyes on Wes he spoke to the man on his left.

'He was the one I told you about, Mr Fisk. Likes to poke his nose in where it's not wanted.' There was a sneer in his voice that was reflected in his eyes.

Wes eyed Cabal Fisk for the first time, seeing a man in his late fifties, early sixties, of medium stature and height with grey, swept-back hair and a neatly trimmed grey beard. Clad in a dark, three-piece suit, light-blue silk shirt and dark-blue cravat, he could easily have passed for a businessman or banker. He regarded Wes with calm, brown eyes set in a lean, not unhandsome, face.

'What do you want here, Mr . . . Mr . . . ?' The voice was cultured and refined, but it was the eyes that held Wes's attention. They were eyes without compassion or mercy. They were the eyes of death itself and Wes found it hard to suppress a shudder beneath the unyielding stare.

'Hardiman, Wes Hardiman. Take a seat, gents, but be sure to keep your hands on the table where I can see 'em otherwise I tend to get a little trigger-happy. You, Bryce, toss the gunbelt into the corner.'

Chairs were quickly righted and the players sat down hands spread out amid the cards and money. With a shrug of his lips Bryce did as Wes commanded.

'Cowboy, you sure are digging yourself a hole an' no mistake,' he drawled.

A smile twitched Wes's lips, but he said nothing. There were three more chairs against the wall behind Wes. Keeping his pistol on the group he dragged one across and sat down.

'Now ain't that cosy?' he said.

'Well, Mr Hardiman, you still haven't answered as to why you are here,' Fisk prompted coldly.

'Just a social chat. Figured it was 'bout time we got acquainted.'

'And just why should I acquaint myself with you?'

'Curiosity, and 'cause your errand boy here,' — he gave Bryce a look — 'might have given the wrong impression o' me.'

Bryce's face reddened, but he said nothing.

'And just what impression do you think I should have of you?' Fisk queried.

'A good friend o' mine disappeared from here a while back. Now if'n I find out that you had anything to do with it, I'll put a bullet between your eyes.' Wes stared hard at Fisk. 'That sort of impression, Mr Fisk.'

7

Tension filled the room following Wes's words. The onlookers could only gape and wonder what Cabal Fisk's reaction would be to the young man's thinly veiled threat.

The two stared silently at each other, the only sound, muted as it came through the wall, of the bar beyond.

Cabal Fisk suddenly threw back his head and laughed, breaking the tension that had thickened unbearably and amusement danced in his eyes as he looked back at Wes.

'You are a refreshingly blunt young man. Yes, Bryce had given me the wrong impression of you, but you have set that right now. Perhaps I can do the same for you about me. Why should I have anything to do with your friend's disappearance?'

'I was told that nothing happened on

the waterfront that you didn't know 'bout.'

'An exaggeration, Mr Hardiman. Of course I get to hear of many things, but that's after they have happened. As to your friend . . . ' Fisk spread his hands in a shrug.

'Ben Travis,' Wes supplied. 'Big man. Once seen never forgotten.'

'The waterfront can be a dangerous place,' Fisk said.

'So I've been told. An old man died earlier this evening. Burnt to death in his cabin.'

'So I heard. Very unfortunate. A tragic accident. Bosun was a character and part of the waterfront. He will be missed.'

'Unfortunate, yes. Tragic, yes. Accident? No, unless his hounds in a fit of remorse shot themselves.'

Fisk frowned. 'I'm afraid I don't understand.'

'Bosun had a couple o' hounds, black as hell an' mean to strangers. They had both been shot. In my book that means someone wanted Bosun outa the way, but afore they could do that they had to get rid o' the hounds. Mighty careless to leave the hounds lying 'bout like that though, they shoulda' got rid o' them, an' everyone, like you said, woulda' called it an accident. Plumb careless o' someone, don't you think?' Wes arched an eyebrow.

'If you say so, Mr Hardiman.' Fisk sounded bored.

'Careless?' Wes pulled a wry face. 'Or mebbe someone so sure o' himself that he thinks he's above the law.'

'An interesting thought. Do you have anybody in mind, Mr Hardiman?' Cabal Fisk locked eyes with Wes in a challenging stare.

Wes shrugged and held the stare. 'I was kinda' hoping you might be able to help me on that one, Mr Fisk.'

'Alas, no one springs immediately to mind.' Fisk sounded almost apologetic.

Wes studied the man for a moment or two. 'Do you know what I think, Mr Fisk?'

Cabal Fisk smiled patiently. 'I'm sure you'll tell us, Mr Hardiman.'

'I think the old man was killed because he spoke to me, so that makes his death kind o' personal an' I'll do anything I can to find out who did it no matter whose toes I tread on in the process. I'm also of a mind that finding the killer or killers will bring me a step closer to finding out what happened to my friend.' Wes climbed to his feet and smiled coldly down at Fisk. 'I'm glad we had this little chat, Mr Fisk, it sorta sets things a mite clearer in my mind.' From the floor behind Wes the guard began to groan his way back to consciousness.

Wes edged his way back to the door still keeping his gun on the group.

'You'll have to let me know if you find out anything,' Fisk called out conversationally.

'Reckon you'll be the first to know,' Wes replied, as he let himself out and closed the door.

Bryce came to his feet and grabbed up his gunbelt.

'I'll take care o' him, Mr Fisk,' Bryce snapped, buckling the gunbelt on as he headed for the door, but Cabal Fisk stopped him.

'I'll tell you when anything or anyone needs taking care of, Bryce,' he said sharply. 'Get rid of that thing on the floor and find someone who can do the job, then sit down. We're here to play poker.' He eyed the other three players who had watched in mesmerized fascination at the word play between the two. 'Shall we continue, gentlemen? My call I believe.'

⋆ ⋆ ⋆

Back at Flynne's, Wes enjoyed a whiskey as he recounted the evening's events to Sean and Siobhan.

'I'd have loved to have been a fly on the wall there,' Sean cried, admiration is his voice ''T'would have been a grand sight to see. What d'yer say, Siobhan?'

'I'm thinking it was a foolish thing to do. You could have been killed.' There was no hero worship in her face, rather the opposite.

'Now is that any way to speak, Siobhan?' Sean admonished curtly and Siobhan tossed her head like a skittish colt.

'Dead heroes are of no use to anyone,' she replied coldly.

Wes laughed. 'It was not meant to be heroic, Miss Flynne. Just a little bit of gentle prodding to show Fisk that he's not in complete control of the situation. Make him worry, because, in my experience, worried men tend to make mistakes.'

She stared at him and her face softened, but the concern remained.

'I hope you know what you are doing, Wes.'

'So do I,' Wes replied soberly, 'an' I think the only way to get to the bottom o' this is to get aboard Fisk's boat the next time it puts to sea an' find out just where it does go.'

'Are you crazy, man?' Sean blurted out, eyes popping.

'Possibly,' Wes agreed calmly.

'You'd play into Fisk's hands if you were discovered,' Siobhan declared.

'I figure the risks are worth taking,' Wes replied, undaunted.

'I don't know,' Sean said unhappily, shaking his head.

'Well, I do. Can you find out when she sails next, Sean?'

'That's no problem. You saw her yourself earlier heading out to sea. Today's Tuesday and like I said before — '

'Every Tuesday and Friday,' Wes cut in. 'That gives us a couple o' days to figure out how to sneak me aboard for the next run.'

* * *

The man died in Ben's arms. He had fallen from the wooden scaffold on to the rock strewn floor below. He could have been no more than twenty years of age, his body beneath the tattered clothes he wore thin and emaciated.

Ben watched the life force fade in his deep-sunk eyes and for an instant before the eyes glazed over, Ben saw a gleam of relief, then it was gone. The head lolled and Ben lowered him gently to the ground as around him the other prisoners gathered like silent ghosts in the shadowy gloom.

Jonas Flagg stared down at the still form. 'At least he is free of this place at last,' he murmured. 'We must get the body to the lift and send it up with the gold. God in Heaven, what was that?' The cry was wrenched from Flagg's lips by a harsh, explosive cracking sound that echoed around the cavern. To Ben's ears it sounded like the crack of a whip.

Dust fell from the darkness above drifting down past the lamps like specks of glistening silver while beneath his feet the floor seemed to quiver.

Ben stared up into the thick, overhead darkness in a purely reflex move for it was impossible to say where the sound came from for it seemed to be all around them. He shook his head as the echoes faded away and were absorbed by the eternal thunder roll of the distant waves and the sudden, rapid beating of his heart.

Jonas Flagg licked his lips, eyes uneasy. 'I don't like the feel of it, shipmate,' he muttered nervously. He looked as though he was about to add to his concern when a weird, multiple whistling filled the cavern, rising in strength until the air about them became filled with a shriek that had them clapping their hands to their ears and sending some to their knees.

Ben remained on his feet hands pressed tight to his ears. Even so the sound burrowed through flesh and bone and into his brain. It was as though the very rocks were screaming in mortal agony.

After what seemed an eternity, but

was only seconds, the sound faded away.

'Holy Mother of God,' Jonas muttered, as he climbed unsteadily to his feet. 'The old seadog ain't never heard the like of it afore. What do you make of it, Ben?'

Ben shook his head as his heart slowed to match the muted boom of the sea.

'I don't know, but I sure got a bad feeling 'bout it.'

No more strange sounds came to disturb them. Ben carried the body of the dead youth to the waiting lift and after loading the gold ore placed the body on top. Jonas had already called up the shaft to alert the guards that a body was being sent up and the two watched as the crude lift creaked and groaned as it was winched up.

After a while when the lift reached the top, Ben heard the distant rattle of gunfire as the waiting guards pumped bullets into the corpse.

'As I said, they like to make sure,'

Jonas voiced. 'Dead is the only way any of us will leave this hell hole!'

★　★　★

From the top of a scrub-covered headland, Wes and Sean looked down into a wide, sandy cove where Cabal Fisk's twin-masted ship, *The Hawk*, was moored at the end of a long, wooden jetty. Lying flat,the two could look down without being seen. Earlier that morning Sean had sailed his single-masted boat, *The Colleen*, along the coast to where *The Hawk* was moored.

In a small neighbouring cove he had dropped anchor, then the two had climbed the cliffs to their present position. In the clear, warm air with the sun on their backs, the voices of the men working the derrick, loading large barrels and sacks into the hold of *The Hawk*, carried to their ears. Sean recognized the sacks as containing grain and flour.

' 'Tis food supplies they are loading,' he whispered to Wes, but he frowned as he spoke.

'What's the matter?' Wes questioned.

' 'Tis the barrels they are loading. I've seen enough of them to know that they are water barrels.'

'And?' Wes shrugged, mystified at Sean's apparent wonder.

'There are so many for such a short journey at sea. Why there must be a hundred or more. I know of no place along this coast where water in such quantity is needed.'

A sudden excitement caused by the other's words gripped Wes.

'Mebbe not along the coast, but what about an island out to sea where there is no fresh water, or perhaps not enough?' The two eyed each other.

'You are thinking of the Isla de la Muerte,' Sean said, and shook his head. 'But why, there is nothing there?' He looked helplessly at Wes.

'It makes sense,' Wes continued with his train of thought. 'Men taken by the

Gatherers are never seen again except the one rescued from the sea who, before he died, spoke of 'men from the sea'. Not seamen, as is generally believed, but as Bosun said, men who arrived from the sea by ship; the Gatherers!'

'The Gatherers live on the island?'

'When more prisoners are required, the Gatherers are brought to the mainland on *The Hawk*. They pick up horses, probably Fisk has a place on the mainland where the horses are stabled. The men and prisoners taken back aboard *The Hawk* which then sails to the island. Prisoners need feeding and watering as do the guards watching over the prisoners.'

'You're going too fast for me, Wes,' Sean protested. 'Prisoners? Guards? Why, 'tis nothing more than a piece of rock rising out of the sea.'

'That's why I need to get aboard *The Hawk* before she sails,' Wes reminded Sean soberly.

''Tis a fool's mission, Wes. What if

you are caught? There's no cavalry to come galloping to the rescue. Why don't we take my boat, *The Colleen*? 'T'will be safer,' Sean offered, but Wes shook his head.

'If the island is being used as I suspect, then they will have lookouts ready to spot any suspicious boat. That being the case, once word gets back to Fisk, it could bring a lot of trouble to Siobhan and yourself. It's better this way.'

Sean shook his head resignedly. 'How then do you hope to get aboard before she sails on the afternoon tide? In broad daylight and with all those men about, 't'will be impossible, that's for sure.'

It was a problem that had been vexing Wes, but one that solved itself. A little after noon, the men working on *The Hawk* stopped their toils as the ringing of a handbell filled the cover, and made their way to a long, single-storey wooden building reminiscent of a ranch bunkhouse and disappeared inside.

'Must be grub time,' Wes announced and smiled grimly. 'I think that's my signal to get aboard.'

'I wish you'd think more about this, Wes,' Sean said worriedly.

'I have an' it's the only way,' Wes replied stubbornly. He caught Sean's hand in a strong grip. 'Thanks for all your help, Sean, you an' Siobhan. We'll have a drink together when I get back.'

Sean smiled, but worry still filled his eyes. 'That we will, my friend. Take care.'

Seconds later, Sean watched as Wes scrambled down the cliff to the sandy beach and ran at a half crouch towards *The Hawk*, his footprints mingling with those already there.

Wes reached the ship without incident. The hatch covers were still open. By means of a wooden ladder, he scrambled down into the hold and spent a few minutes rearranging grain sacks in one dark corner to hollow out a hiding place. Then, with heart beating fast and a tautness in his stomach, he settled down to wait. It was hot and airless and sweat dappled his face. He had brought a canteen of water with him and was glad he had.

The wait seemed interminable, but finally he heard men's voices. Footsteps rattled on the decking above. Two men descended into the hold and Wes drew his gun, but the men were not looking for unexpected guests. They were there to stow the last of the cargo that was being lowered into the hold.

After the men had departed, the hatch covers were closed and bolted into position and Wes was on his own, the first part of his plan accomplished. All he could do now was wait.

The hatch covers were made up of wooden mesh panels that allowed some light to penetrate the gloom of the hold, something for which Wes was grateful. It was a long wait, but finally *The Hawk* was underway. He climbed stiffly from his hiding place and stretched his cramped limbs.

Later he lay back on the grain sacks in the stifling, semi-darkness and listened to the creak of timbers and slap of the sea on the hull. He had no definite plan in mind for when *The Hawk* reached its destination, but something would turn up, he hoped!

★   ★   ★

Ben was on the top platform of the wooden scaffold chipping away at the vein of gold ore when a sudden commotion to one side of the cavern made him pause. Jonas Flagg appeared at the bottom of the scaffold, face turned up in his direction, lantern in his hand.

'What's going on?' Ben called down. He could see fear etched into the other's lamp-lit features.

'Water! There's a pool o' water appeared over there.' He indicated into the darkness. ''T'was not there yester-day.'

'So?' Ben was not yet aware of the

possible meaning of the discovery.

'It's salt water, shipmate. The sea's getting in an' that ain't a sight I'm wanting to see,' Jonas wailed back.

Ben lay aside his pick and clambered down to the other's side.

'Show me.'

He followed Jonas taking a parallel course with the work face until they reached the corner and, in the flickering glow of Jonas's lantern, a deep pool of water had formed in a rocky depression on the floor. Even as the two watched the water spilled over into a second depression.

'It's bad, very bad,' Jonas said, hoarsely, running a grimy hand over his lips. 'Once the sea finds a way in she ain't satisfied until she claims everything for Davey Jones's Locker, including us poor souls.'

'Then let's make sure them gents up top know,' Ben said decisively, grabbing Jonas's arm and steering him towards the shaft. They had covered about half the distance when the cavern became filled with a low, moaning wail that stopped the two in their tracks.

'What in tarnation?' Ben cried.

A series of multiple whistling similar to those they had heard earlier played a discordant note, then, with a thunderous crack, a section of the floor between them and the wooden scaffold opened up sending a hissing, roaring column of white water into the air and instantly the whistling stopped.

It was then Ben realized what had caused the whistling sound. Tunnels, either natural or man made, beneath the cavern, had been breeched, and the incoming sea was forcing the air out through tiny cracks and crevices, the pressure making it 'sing' as it were.

The column of water hit the high roof with tremendous force. Broken fragments of stalactite began to rain down from out of the darkness above the two accompanied by a torrent of spray that fell with the savageness of a summer storm.

Drenched to the skin, the two raced

towards the base of the shaft in a purely reflex action. They had barely reached its cone of light when an ear splitting roar shook the cavern. Ben turned and his eyes widened in fear as the work face exploded outwards to be replaced by a surging, foaming wall of water.

Just before the lanterns were ripped from their places and doused, Ben saw the wooden scaffold break apart and the timbers carried forward, like lances in a cavalry charge. Then darkness obscured the terrible sight, but it could not hide the sound, a roar, like a train in a mountain tunnel, as the wall of water rushed towards himself and Jonas Flagg.

8

In the circle of light that flowed down the shaft, the two men stared up desperately. From the lip of the shaft high above, tiny heads were looking down. Jonas screamed at them to lower the platform, but his cries were lost in the growing hiss and rumble of the water rushing through the darkness towards them.

Ben knew that there would be no time to lower the platform. He cast a look into the inky blackness and his heart froze as a wall of foaming white appeared on the edge of the cone of light. In one single, awful second, he saw the mass of boiling, churning water carrying within it the timbers from the scaffold that turned and twisted in the watery grip along with the bodies of the other prisoners.

'Jonas!' he bellowed, turning and

throwing himself against the wall, spreadeagling his arms and curling his fingers around whatever tenuous handholds he could feel. A split second later, the water rammed into his body like the kick of a mule, almost driving the hastily sucked in air from his lungs.

The force of the water pinned him against the rock wall, driving his head forward against the unyielding surface. Pain exploded through his skull. He almost lost consciousness, only the coldness of the water keeping him awake.

Jonas Flagg was not so lucky. A heavy timber pole caught the screaming man full in the face, driving him back against the rock wall and crushing his head to a pulp and killing him instantly.

The horrifying end to Jonas Flagg happened within a few yards of Ben, but the big man knew nothing of it as he fought his own battle for survival.

Timbers and bodies hit the wall all around Ben. Something slammed him hard across the shoulders and then was gone leaving agony in its wake. He could only guess that it was probably a piece of timber, perhaps one of the cage props.

Grimly he clung on as the motion of the water changed and began to surge in a huge spiral, turning back on itself to meet with the water still pouring in. It tried to tear him from the wall, but he held on doggedly, knowing that if he lost his grip now he would be swept back into the cavern and certain death.

He did not know how long he could hold his breath for, but already his lungs were beginning to burn. He lifted his head and opened his eyes snapping them shut instantly as the sand and grit-filled water stung his eyes. Cautiously he partially opened them again. Above him a milky opalescence indicated the distant surface of the water-filled shaft, criss-crossed with slowly spinning timbers and the broken bodies of the other prisoners.

Bubbles of precious air dribbled from his lips as the terrible burning in his lungs increased. The spinning, whirling current had lost its strength, the clawing drag reduced to little more than a soft caress now that the cavern had filled with water.

Lights danced in Ben's eyes, swirling sparks of colour. Air began to trickle from his lips in a steady stream that he could no longer hold back. He released his finger-cramped grip and felt himself floating away from the wall.

Panic gripped him and he pushed upwards towards the circle of murky light kicking with his feet. The effort drove the remainder of the air from his lungs. The desire to open his mouth and breathe in was overpowering, but somehow, summoning up the last vestiges of will power, he kept his mouth closed and clamped his nose with numb fingers.

He was on the verge of passing out when his head broke the surface of the water amid a tangle of broken and splintered timbers and he sucked in a massive gulp of air. His arms shot out and wrapped themselves around a piece of timber and he clung on, gulping in more air, his head clearing, the dancing, coloured lights fading from his vision.

He could hear voices coming from above and, looking up, he was surprised to see the underneath of the platform less than ten feet above. The platform hid him from the owners of the voices and instinct told him to remain hidden. He used his feet to keep himself beneath the platform and away from prying eyes and it saved his life.

As bodies appeared on the surface of the water, the crash of gunshots filled the air and the bodies jerked as bullets tore into them.

One prisoner who had somehow survived the watery death, waved an arm weakly and called for help in a voice hardly more than a whisper. His reply was a bullet in the head followed by a wave of coarse laughter from above.

A dark, savage anger surged through Ben and he vowed then and there that he would avenge the man's death and the deaths of all the others who had perished in the Devil's Ladle, but his own troubles were far from over.

The icy chill of the water was sapping the strength from his body, already numb with cold, and only his grip on the piece of timber kept him from slipping beneath the water. His teeth chattered in his head and he prayed the guards would soon tire of their sport and move away leaving him the opportunity to escape from the shaft. The wall of the shaft, from what he could see of it, looked climbable, if his body could make it, but the longer he stayed in the water so his chances diminished.

The motion of the water had ceased and the shattered remains of the wooden scaffold had gathered around him, nudging at his bruised and battered body. He tried to rest on two logs, but the second spun away colliding with another before drifting into the open.

'Did you hear that?' a voice from above exclaimed. 'There's something under the platform!'

Ben's heart froze.

'Could be someone still alive,' a second voice said.

'Then let's lower the platform. Anyone under it will have to come out or drown.'

Ben's heart began to beat faster as he listened to the voices then heard the creak of the winch. He looked up and saw with horror the platform slowly descending towards him. He had a choice: drown or be shot!

★   ★   ★

Wes snapped awake suddenly. The warmth of the hold combined with the rocking motion of the boat had had a soporific effect on him sending him into a doze. He sat up groggily shaking his head to clear it.

The motion of the boat had changed, the rocking more pronounced, and above the creak of the timbers he could hear the thunder of waves breaking on rocks. Feet rattled on the deckboards above his head and he could hear men shouting. A tightness settled in his stomach and his heart began to pump. Had they fouled the deadly reefs that surrounded the Isla de la Muerte? He could do nothing but wait with pounding heart, fearful that at any moment the hull would splinter and tear apart and the sea rush in.

Above deck, hidden from his eyes, seaman shortened sail as *The Hawk* negotiated the narrow and only passage through the reefs to the island. *The Hawk* dipped and swayed, bucking like a skittish mare through a sea that boiled and foamed, the waves breaking in gigantic fans of white spray against the rocks, the spray floating down to cover the deck and rails in a slick of moisture.

At the wheel, Captain Hollister smiled through a silver beard. A seaman of many years' experience, the narrow channel presented no fears for him. In fact it was the opposite, he enjoyed the challenge as *The Hawk* nosed into deep troughs then reared on foaming crests. Feet braced apart, calloused hands gripping the spokes of the wheel, he kept the boat on an even course that would bring it into the calm bay that fronted the island.

Beyond the flying spray, black cliffs rose sheer and inhospitable to the deep blue of the sky and the delicate, shimmering arc of a rainbow. Moisture dripped from the shiny peak of the captain's cap and sparkled in his beard.

Moisture dripped through carved mesh of the hatch covers alarming Wes and adding to his fear that the boat was on the verge of sinking. The crashing of the waves on the rocks beyond the hull filled the hold with a constant boom and Wes was forced to return to his cramped hideaway to save himself from being thrown about as the ship rose and fell.

The boards beneath his feet shuddered and groaned as the boat dropped into deep troughs, wallowed sluggishly before the next wave sent it flying forward and upward in a stomach-churning surge. With pounding heart, Wes braced himself and waited.

★　★　★

With a sickening feeling of defeat, Ben watched the platform descend towards him. He had been in many tight spots in his life, but none to equal this where hope had completely and utterly deserted him.

There was a commotion in the water near the centre of the flooded shaft that sent waves rippling outwards to slap noisily at the shaft walls. A voice called out for the winch to be stopped and the platform came to a halt a mere two feet above his head.

'There was something there,' a voice called out, and then suddenly the water exploded upwards in a fountain of spray. Something big and silver flashed and then was gone. The timber sections around Ben grouped together noisily and slammed into his body.

Ben fought back a cry of pain then his eyes caught sight of something dark and triangular, like the sail on a child's toy coat, cleaving the water. It was heading for a corpse floating on the water. As he watched, part of a huge silvery body emerged above the water. He saw a mouth ringed with savage, pointed teeth, a single dark, emotionless eye, then the corpse was grabbed and with a tremendous splash both corpse and fish were gone.

'Hey, Brogan, it's a goddamn shark!' Ben heard a voice proclaim.

'Must'a got dragged in when the water entered the cavern,' the man called Brogan explained.

Ben had heard of sharks and the merciless killing machines that they were, but this was the first time he had ever seen one.

The fin of the shark reappeared

cutting an erratic pattern. Zigzagging across the centre of the shaft then circling close to the edge of the platform. Ben felt that it could sense him and was just waiting for the opportunity to move in. With a sweep of its tail, the shark disappeared beneath the water.

'*The Hawk*'s on the way in!' a new voice called out excitedly, as another person joined the group above. There was a muttered curse at the news, then, 'I'll get down to the jetty. Word is that Mr Fisk is on board an' he'll wanna know about this as soon as possible. Look lively, you men, check the other tunnels.' It was Brogan's voice.

Ben held his breath and waited, ears pricked. He heard a general grumble go up and then the sound of booted feet retreating away from the edge of the shaft. Silence enveloped him interrupted only by the slap of water against rock, then a splashing sound attracted his attention as the shark resurfaced.

Ben watched the fin cleaving the

water as the shark circled restlessly, sensing him, but hampered by the debris of floating timbers from reaching the man.

Ben pushed some of the timbers out hoping to confuse the shark more than it was confused now. The lowering of the platform offered Ben a real means of escape, but the circling shark lessened the possibility. He sent a few more timbers floating out across the water.

The water seethed and churned in the centre as the snout of the shark appeared. It opened a gaping maw ringed with the razor-sharp teeth and in one savage snap, bit clean through a section of broken timber, shearing it in half, before diving below the surface.

Timbers knocked together in the choppy water. Ben realized his only chance for survival was to give the shark something else to think about and quickly too for he was weakening rapidly in the chill water.

He selected a six-foot length of

timber, three inches in diameter, the end splintered to half its thickness forming a rudimentary spear. With one hand capping the thicker, rear end of the timber, the other a foot or so along it, he propelled himself forward and out into the open.

The shark was on the far side of the shaft, now it turned and moved towards him at great speed, snout lifting as its mouth gaped open. Ben lifted the improvised spear a few inches. He knew that he would only get one chance. If he failed he would be torn to pieces. He shut the thought from his mind and focused himself. With all the might he could muster, he thrust the splintered end into the shark's open mouth driving it deep into flesh and muscle.

The shark's impetus pushed Ben back under the platform, ramming him hard against the floating timbers as the improvised spear was torn from his grip by the shark's agonized threshing about. Blood erupted from its mouth, staining the water before the mouth snapped shut severing the timber in half.

The shark went wild with the piece of timber firmly lodged in its throat. It rolled and writhed, dived down then surfaced in a dramatic explosion of water and spray. The silver flash of its body arched in the tormented fans of agitated, flying water tinged red with its own blood that pumped from its grey, leathery lips.

Sending out all the timbers to further impede the maddened beast, Ben made his move. He reached up, grabbed the edge of the platform and hauled his numb body on to the rough planking. He dragged himself to its centre and, rolling on to his back lay still: exhausted. His movements caused the platform to swing gently, ropes creaking softly.

He could hear the shark thrashing about, the timbers clattering together, but soon the sounds grew less and finally stopped altogether and a warm peace enveloped him.

Aboard *The Hawk*, as suddenly as it had begun, the violent motion of the boat ceased and the booming noise fell away aft.

From above, a ragged cheer went up from the throats of the crew as it did every trip following the successful passage through the channel. It was a cheer that Wes could have gladly lent a voice to, but he had to content himself with a silent cheer of relief.

The Hawk glided through the still waters of a deep bay towards a long, T-shaped jetty that marched out on wooden legs from a lip of sandy beach into the sea. Ten minutes later, *The Hawk* bumped gently against the head of the T and ropes were thrown to waiting men who turned them around heavy, wooden capstans. *The Hawk* had arrived.

Wes, feeling slightly nauseous from the buffeting he had taken, pressed himself back into his hiding place as the hatch covers were opened and light flooded into the hold. He pulled his Colt and eased back the hammer, ready for whatever fate had in store for him. But then something happened that he was not ready for and it left him completely stunned.

'You can come out now, Mr Hardiman, the voyage is over.' It was the voice of Cabal Fisk.

9

'Come, Mr Hardiman, Wes, don't be shy,' Fisk called again, amusement in his voice. 'Please leave your weapons there. My men are well armed and provocation on your part will only hasten your own end.'

The bitterness of defeat swept through Wes. He tossed his gun out and clambered stiffly from his hiding place. A half-dozen men, dressed in western style with rifles pointed at him, lined the hatch above. Fisk was not in view, no doubt covering his bets just in case Wes decided to come out shooting. He clambered over the sacks and climbed the ladder to the deck.

Cabal Fisk stood with the bearded captain, smiling broadly as Wes came into view.

'I trust you had a pleasant journey, Wes?' Fisk jeered.

'How did you know I was on board?'

'You were being watched. When you and your meddlesome friend set out, word was sent to me. You were watched all the way to the cover by clifftop look-outs. You were even watched as you watched us and *The Hawk* was deliberately deserted to allow you to sneak aboard. It was all too easy,' Fisk smirked.

'Guess you can't win 'em all,' Wes said flatly.

'Not in my world you can't,' Fisk replied arrogantly.

'What is your world, Fisk? What's on this island that you need men for?'

'Gold, Wes. I found it by accident when I was ship-wrecked here some years ago, but not any gold. This is very special gold and a special place that men have searched for ever since the Spanish invaded.'

'Do I get to hear more?' Wes prompted.

'As you will soon be digging that gold out for me it's only fair that you should know about the Isla de la Muerte. Incidentally your friend — Ben wasn't it? — well, he's here and will no doubt be overjoyed to see you.'

'Get on with it, Fisk,' Wes said through grated teeth.

'Have you ever heard of the Incas, Wes?' Fisk arched an eyebrow and toyed with his trim, neat beard.

'Bunch o' South American Indians that the Spanish killed.'

'I'm impressed,' Fisk acknowledged. 'Well, the Incas had a number of gold and silver mines, but there was always talk of one particular gold mine, a fabulously wealthy, 'lost' mine that men have been trying to find for years. This place is it. The Isla de la Muerte is the lost gold mine of the Incas.'

Wes frowned as he searched his memory for childhood facts.

'I heard these Incas lived in the mountains an' didn't go to sea.'

'Quite right, Wes, you do surprise me. But the Incas were friends of the coastal Indians who did, and it was these who found the island. How or why will always remain a mystery, but I'm glad they did for I was able to rediscover it.'

'Hence the men you needed for the Gatherers to collect them?'

Cabal Fisk clapped his hands slowly together.

'Excellent, Wes. You have the whole story. It's just unfortunate, from your point of view, that you will never have anyone to tell it to.'

'Don't be too sure, Fisk. The people I work for are mighty persistent at getting to the truth.'

'All taken care of,' Fisk replied with a shrug. He turned his head and raised his voice. 'Wouldn't you say so, Sheriff?'

'That I would, Mr Fisk. I took care of everything myself.'

Wes's head snapped around and a look of dumb-founded surprise filled his eyes as Sheriff Russell emerged from below decks and strode arrogantly to Fisk's side, smiling eyes on Wes.

The look on Wes's face increased Fisk's amusement.

'You don't seriously think that I'd let some petty, cowtown outfit out-think and outsmart me, do you, Wes? And if you are thinking of saying, 'You'll never get away with it, Fisk', tell him, Sheriff.'

'I've sent a wire to your Colonel Paxton offering my sincere condolences over your unfortunate, but very brave, death in attempting to rescue Bosun from his burning cabin. I need just a couple more items to add that touch of authenticity.' He nodded to the nearest of the ring of men. 'His hat and gunbelt. By the way, Wes, meet the Gatherers.' He indicated the circle of grinning men as Wes's hat was snatched from his head and his gunbelt removed.

'I'm sure to 'member you boys,' Wes promised darkly.

'You have a comforting sense of optimism in the face of overwhelming adversity. I like that in a man, Wes,' Fisk called out. 'So much better than whining and pleading. Your partner had that same bravado, though I doubt he has it now.'

'You ain't gonna fool the colonel that easily,' Wes opined.

'We'll burn the hat and gunbelt a little. Not too much, but enough to make them still recognizable to the colonel. Might even take a trip to Tucson and deliver them in person,' Russell nodded.

'Well I think it's time we reunited you with your long, lost friend, Wes. I'm sure you'll both have a lot to talk about.'

'What happened to Jacob?' Wes asked abruptly.

Cabal Fisk smiled. 'He is learning the error of his ways. Like you, he is stubborn, but our Señor Cardonna, The Bull, as he is called, has a way of converting stubborn to craven, as you will find out. Take him away now.' His eyes never left Wes's face as he issued the order. 'Goodbye, Mr Hardiman. We will not meet again.'

Wes smiled coldly. 'Mebbe, mebbe not. You an' the sheriff there had better pray that it's the mebbe not.'

Rifle barrels were poked sharply into his body as, with hands in the air, he was marched off *The Hawk* and escorted down the long, wooden jetty by three of the Gatherers.

Desperate thoughts of escape were running through Wes's brain, each of them ending in the unpleasant sight of his own body riddled with bullets, when Fate leant a hand.

A guard from the mine, sweating and blowing from the exertion of running, appeared at the mouth of a wide ravine that led inwards and upwards from the cove. He lurched across the lip of sand and staggered on to the welcome, solid boards of the jetty, cuffing sweat from his eyes.

He hardly seemed to notice Wes and his three armed escorts as he staggered, regained his feet and charged towards them. His mission was to get to Mr Fisk with the news of the mine collapse.

'Outa the way!' he gasped hoarsely. 'Big trouble at the mine.'

Wes had a man on each side of him

and another bringing up the rear. As the guard from the mine began pushing his way through, Wes saw his chance.

The escort to Wes's left sidestepped, eyes fixed angrily on the charging man. Wes stepped to his right and turned as the guard pushed past, lunging into the escort on his right. Like the other two, all eyes were on the sweating, breathless man. Wes grasped the rifle barrel of the distracted escort, pulled it from his grip and drove the wooden stock into the man's surprised face.

Bone and wood met with a sickening crunch. The man cried out in agony as his nose exploded in a blossom of red. He staggered sideways, lost his footing and tumbled from the jetty into the water.

As the escort fell, Wes, now facing towards *The Hawk* put a foot into the small of the passing mine guard's back and sent him lurching into the rear escort. Both men crashed down in a sprawling, yelling heap.

During the move, Wes kept the rifle

swinging. It caught the remaining man, who had sidestepped earlier, under the chin and sent him flying from the jetty.

Wes, heart pumping, adrenalin surging, dropped to one knee, reversing the rifle and firing as his knee hit wood.

The rear escort who had untangled himself from the mine guard, was up in a half crouch, rifle levelled. He cried out as the bullet smashed through his ribs and into his right lung, blowing a fist-sized exit hole just below his right shoulder-blade.

The bullet half turned him in his tracks. Blood erupted from his mouth. He attempted to turn the rifle and himself in Wes's direction, but his legs were buckling beneath him. He went heavily to his knees. The rifle exploded as death throes twitched his finger and blew a hole in the jetty boards. He dropped the rifle as he toppled forward.

The luckless mine guard who had started the ruckus, fearing he was next to be shot, threw himself from the jetty.

Wes, who had already levered another

shell into the breech of the rifle, now fired at *The Hawk* and surprised faces disappeared as the men aboard dived for cover.

The whole sequence of events had taken less than ten seconds. Tucking the rifle he had used under his left arm, he grabbed up the dead man's rifle in his left hand. Precious seconds were then lost as he drew a Navy Colt from the dead-man's holster and thumbed the hammer back. He decided that if he was going on the run he needed as much firepower as he could get. Taking it now, while they were still stunned, was the only chance he was likely to get.

Heads had appeared above the rail of *The Hawk*, but vanished quickly again as he fired the Colt and began to back rapidly down the jetty.

He fired three times before reaching the end, then turned, and, at a crouch, ran at an angle across the sand.

He did not head for the ravine at the rear of the cove. The mine guard had arrived from that direction indicating to Wes that that was the main route to the mine. If the shots had been heard that would be the way others would come to investigate.

Instead, his keen eyes had picked out a narrow gully leading up the cliffs to the right, and it was towards this he headed.

A rattle of rifle shots sounded from *The Hawk* and bullets buzzed around him like angry bees. One struck a rock and whined eerily away into the lengthening shadows as the evening sun dropped towards the western horizon. Wes dived full length behind a rock at the start of the gully and rolled on to his back, breathing heavily. Bullets chipped at the rock, but for the moment he was safe.

On board *The Hawk*, Fisk shouted, 'Stop shooting!' He rose cautiously to his feet, a grudging smile on his face. The men at the rail with guns looked questioningly at him. 'Mr Hardiman is a resourceful and audacious young man. I like that,' he murmured.

'But he's got away,' Sheriff Russell cried out, a hint of panic in his voice that caused Fisk to raise a questioning eyebrow.

'Got away to where, Sheriff? There is nowhere to go on the island. On the contrary, it will be fun hunting him.' He looked at the men on the rail. 'You are called the Gatherers. Then go and gather. Bring him back dead and you can share a thousand dollars between you. Bring him back alive and you will get a thousand dollars each.'

As the men scrambled to get off *The Hawk*, Russell turned angrily to Fisk.

'Just what in tarnation are you playing at, Fisk?'

'I don't play at anything, Mr Russell. I intend to teach this ignorant cowboy that he is no match for me. Well, Brogan?' He barked.

By now Brogan, the mine guard who had caused all the trouble, appeared, wet and bedraggled, at the rail. He winced at the tone of Fisk's voice.

'It's the mine, Mr Fisk. The sea's broken into the Devil's Ladle. It's flooded to the top of the shaft.'

★   ★   ★

Ben must have fallen asleep. He had no idea for how long, it could have been minutes or hours, though he doubted the latter, but suddenly he jerked awake. He had no idea what had awoken him, but he was instantly alert. He rose stiffly to his feet. His body ached, but he felt better after the brief rest.

Beneath his feet the platform creaked. Below that, the water was still, clogged with shattered timbers, broken bodies and the body of the shark. It floated on its back, pale belly shining dully.

Ben eyed it and shivered before turning and clambering the five feet on to the lip of the water-filled shaft. He crouched there for a few seconds, peering around. The huge cavern he

154

now found himself in with its tunnels leading away to other shafts appeared deserted. The light flooding in through the far entrance was tinged with red; deep shadows were beginning to creep away from the walls.

Ben moved into the shadows and headed towards the entrance. He guessed that night was coming. He passed a tunnel mouth and heard men's voices echoing back along it. The guards were in there overseeing their particular section. He moved on swiftly. He assumed that the guards would soon be emerging from their tunnels to eat and he wanted to be away before he was spotted.

He reached the entrance and paused and saw a sight that made his blood run cold. The frame that had held him, for what seemed an eternity ago now, was again occupied. A huge black man sagged in the ropes that tethered his wrists and ankles. His head hung down on his chest. Before him strutted Ortez Cardonna, The Bull.

The big, bloated Mexican circled the tethered man, the whip trailing in his wake.

'It ees time to wake up, *señor*,' Cardonna's coarse, throaty voice floated back to Ben. There were two other men with The Bull. They had rifles slung over their shoulders to indicate they were guards, not prisoners.

One of the men picked up a bucket of water and threw it over the man bringing him out of the peaceful unconscious state into the agony of reality. His chest was cross-crossed with bloody stripes. He shook his woolly head and glared down at The Bull.

Ortez Cardonna stared back and laughed, displayed his yellow, stained teeth behind thick lips.

'It ees good you be awake, *señor*. I have pain for you, mucho pain. You have no tongue, soon you have no skin.'

Ben's great hands clenched and unclenched as he watched and listened. All three men had their backs to him and it would be easy to slip from the mine into a thicket of trees, he remembered, that lay just a short distance to the right of the entrance. He didn't like the thought of leaving the man to die, but to try and take on three men, all armed, was suicide.

Ben had suffered a lot to gain his freedom. To be shot down whilst attempting a bravado rescue would not help him or the other prisoners.

He was about to slip out of the entrance when the sound of distant gunshots rattled on the air.

Cardonna eyed the two men, frowning a little. He was about to dismiss the shots, when a further, more insistent fusillade, crackled. Cardonna knew that *The Hawk* had come in. Mebbe it had more prisoners and they were trying to escape? He indicated for the two men with him to go and find out before turning his attention back to the prisoner.

Ben's heart leapt as he saw the two men disappear. Whatever the reason for the gunshots, they gave him the chance he had been waiting for. Oblivious to the sharp stones that dug cruelly into the soles of his bare feet, Ben darted from the safety of the mine entrance and sprinted towards Cardonna and his prisoner.

Cardonna was taunting the prisoner. Jacob stared down at the man, his dark eyes filled with hatred, then he caught sight of the half-naked, approaching man and stared with disbelief.

For the first few seconds Cardonna failed to realize that Jacob was staring not at him, but beyond him.

'Mebbe I will cut your . . . ' He stopped, frowning up at the round, dark face and then, at the last minute, he heard the soft slap of feet from behind. He turned as Ben launched a shoulder charge that caught the Mexican squarely in the chest.

Ortez Cardonna, The Bull, flew backwards, surprise registering on his olive features. Seconds later, the surprise became a mask of pain as he slammed against a thick upright of the frame. The frame shook. His eyes shut for a split second, air whooshing from his mouth.

He sagged against the upright then his eyes snapped open. The move had sent Ben to his knees. As he rose to his feet, The Bull let out a roar, shook his head and straightened. The whip was still clasped in his hand. He lashed out and the whip curled itself around Ben's upper body, trapping his arms.

The Bull laughed, the pain mask slipping from his fat face.

'You cannot beat me, *señor*. I am The Bull,' he roared with pride.

With the whip wrapped around his upper arms, Ben could still move his lower arms. He moved forwards, closed his left hand around the whip and yanked hard and savagely.

The handle of the whip flew from the Mexican's grip and Ben shook himself free from its coils. The Bull, still grinning, drew a vicious-looking, broad-bladed knife from a sheath and advanced confidently on the other.

'I cut your heart out, Yankee cowboy,' he grated.

'You can sure try, 'breed,' Ben replied.

The Bull's face darkened at the slur as the two circled. For a big, seemingly overweight, man he moved with remarkable speed and grace, flipping the knife from one hand to the other.

He sliced sideways, the gleaming blade only just missing Ben as the big Texan jolted back. The Bull tossed the knife, caught it in his other hand and scythed out again. This time it caught Ben on the upper left arm, slicing open the skin.

The Mexican hooted out his delight.

'You cannot beat me, gringo. They call me The Bull; not because I am big, but I use the knife like a bull uses its horns. Fast, quick, left, right. Into the hilt when the time is right.'

Ben's beating heart quickened a pace. He had never before come up against a man as quick and proficient with a knife. He changed hands so quickly that it was difficult to know which hand the knife would be in when he struck.

Ben backed, face grim; the Mexican followed him, the knife flying from hand to hand in a blur of silver.

'How you wanna die, gringo?' The Bull taunted and at the same time feinted with his left hand to draw Ben's eyes away from a stabbing lunge with his right.

The Bull was fast, but this time Ben held his ground. The Mexican favoured the right hand and Ben reckoned the killing blow would come from that. He was right. He swung his left forearm down, parrying the thrust while his right forearm swung upwards, slapping the empty hand aside before returning, fist bunched, slamming it against the side of the Mexican's jaw.

The blow staggered The Bull back. Ben moved in, driving a knee into The Bull's groin. The Bull's eyes popped. He stopped still, knees coming together. He tried to lunge with the knife, but it was a slow, unco-ordinated move.

Ben caught the man's wrist and twisted. The Bull let out a hoarse screech as Ben swung the arm outwards and then down on to his rising knee. The Bull's elbow snapped noisily and the screech became a scream of agony. The knife fell from his fingers as he went to his knees, face grey.

Ben picked up the knife, leaving the man kneeling on the ground moaning and holding his shattered arm. He moved across to the prisoner.

'Looks to me like you need a friend, fella. Guess I'm that friend.' Ben slashed the ankle ropes first then the wrist ropes and Jacob swayed heavily in his supporting arms. 'Hell, boy, you weigh some,' Ben croaked. 'Reckon you need to sit a spell.' He gently lowered Jacob to the ground so that his back was against an upright. 'Take few minutes; I know what this damn thing can do to a man.'

Jacob's eyes suddenly widened. He lifted a shaking arm, pointing, and Ben turned.

The Bull, face contorted in rage and pain, had released his injured arm and from somewhere had produced a small, double-barrelled derringer and was pointing it at Ben, finger whitening on his trembling hand as he began to squeeze the trigger.

10

Ben reacted instinctively. He threw the knife at the Mexican in a desperate effort to deflect the other's wavering aim. In the event, his aim was truer and far more deadly than he could have hoped for.

The blade of the heavy knife entered The Bull's right eye and drove itself deep into his brain, killing him instantly and he toppled forward without firing a shot.

Ben limped across and dragged the boots from the dead man's feet.

'My needs are sure greater than yours, Bull,' he muttered, as he forced his feet into the fancy boots, grimacing as they pinched and squeezed his toes. 'Dammit! For a big fella you sure had small feet.'

He took the derringer from The Bull's lifeless hand and returned to Jacob.

'I reckon you can't speak, fella, but can you hear an' understand?' Jacob nodded, eyes on Ben, as the other dropped into a crouch before him. 'We'uns have gotta get moving pronto. Do you think you can walk?' Jacob nodded again and Ben hauled the man to his feet.

Jacob's face contorted with pain. His tongueless mouth opened in a silent scream of agony. The Bull had been merciless. Lash marks covered Jacob's front, back, arms and legs and, as he forced himself to move, blood began to seep from the cuts.

Ben could only feel for the man who was unable to give audible release to his agony. After a few tottery steps, Jacob sank wearily to his knees. Ben's keen ears picked up the sound of voices coming from the direction in which The Bull's henchmen had disappeared earlier.

The shadows were thickening now as the sun balanced itself delicately on the western horizon sending a path of red fire across the sea to bathe the west-facing cliffs in a Hadean glow.

'We gotta go. Men are coming,' Ben whispered urgently to Jacob, but the man shook his head and made gestures that he, Ben, should go and leave him, but Ben shook his head. 'Sorry, fella, we both go,' Ben said, and slammed a fist hard into the other's jaw. Jacob dropped and Ben wasted no time. He hauled the unconscious man up, got a shoulder into his middle and straightened up.

Ben's leg and back muscles threatened to explode under the weight of the huge man. He gritted his teeth and with as much speed as he could muster, headed for the tree thicket.

* * *

As, unknown to Wes, Ben fought with The Bull, Wes scrambled up the steep, narrow gully. At the top he paused to look back. The Gatherers had already reached the end of the jetty and were ploughing across the sand to the gully.

Wes hunkered down low, dropping one rifle before levering a cartridge into the breech of the other and waited.

It wasn't long before he heard cursing voices. He gave a humourless smile, levelled the rifle and as the first head appeared below him, squeezed the trigger.

The luckless man's face exploded like a ripe melon sending him crashing back into those following behind. The gully was narrow and the man's body blocked it. Wes heard voices shouting, 'Back! Git back.' He didn't wait to hear any more. Behind him the ground shelved down into a long, narrow, thickly wooded valley. Grabbing up the second rifle Wes slithered down the stony slope and vanished into the trees.

* * *

Cabal Fisk and Sheriff Russell accompanied by the captain watched the dejected return of the men who had pursued Wes. Two of them carried the dead man between them.

'Sorry, Mr Fisk, he got away,' the lead man, Clay Rutters, a lean, sour-faced man in black, mumbled apologetically.

'There is nowhere he can go. It'll be dark soon. Start looking for him at first light. Post some guards by the gully, and, Captain,' — he swung round to face Captain Hollister — 'Keep look-outs posted on *The Hawk*. Hardiman is not to be underestimated.'

'He'll not get aboard *The Hawk*, Mr Fisk.'

Fisk turned his attention to Russell, the latter still wearing a dark, troubled expression, and laughed.

'You worry too much, Russell. Let's go to the mine. I'm sure Cardonna can offer us some entertainment, in his own, unique style,' Fisk chuckled as he led off across the sand.

Wes's escape had not bothered him in the least; in fact, he was rather glad in a way for it gave an extra element of interest and excitement to the otherwise dull trip. He felt a tingle of anticipation at the thought of when Wes was captured and his own hand administered the insolent cowboy's slow demise.

Cabal Fisk's light-heartedness lasted the twenty minutes it took to trek to the mine.

He stared down at the dead body of Ortez Cardonna, lit now by half-a-dozen kerosene lamps in the hands of the silent guards. Night had fallen and with it a rising moon painted the area in a ghostly, silver glow. As Sheriff Russell viewed the body he could not prevent the sly jibe at Fisk's expense.

'Yes, sir. Old Ortez sure does know how to entertain.' The remark earned him a dirty look from Fisk whose good mood had now turned sour.

'How did this happen?' he thundered at the ring of guards, but there was no response from the frightened faces.

'Whoever did it must have been real strong,' Russell mused. 'Mebbe the

Nigger got free?' He eyed Fisk, but the other shook his head.

'The ropes that held Jacob have been cut, probably with Cardonna's own knife, the same knife that was used to kill him.'

'There's no man alive who could take The Bull's knife from him, let alone use it on him,' Russell objected.

'Are you proposing that Cardonna did it to himself?' Fisk snapped sarcastically.

'What I meant was — '

'It doesn't matter what you meant,' Fisk cut in. 'The truth lies at your feet. Cardonna is dead by his own knife, the prisoner gone. Now who on this island would be capable of such a deed? More to the point: where are they now?' Fisk fumed.

'Who was the last here to see The Bull alive?' Russell asked, eyes raking the semicircle of guards. Two men shambled forward.

'Guess we were,' the thinner of the two spoke up. 'Me an' Pete here were with him until we heard the shooting. Then he sends us off to find out what's going on. When we got back, ten, mebbe fifteen minutes later he was dead an' the Nigger gone.'

Russell stared savagely at the two without saying anything, then turned back to Fisk.

'I don't get it.'

Fisk looked thoughtful, holding his bearded chin and stroking his lips with a finger.

'There is only one prisoner on this island, big and strong enough to have taken on Cardonna, but that would have been impossible. Where was the big Texan put to work?'

'He was taken to the Devil's Ladle as soon as The Bull had finished with him,' a voice replied.

'He was there all the time?'

'No one comes out of there alive, Mr Fisk, an' now he's dead anyway. The Devil's Ladle is flooded with water to near the top of the shaft. They's all dead who worked the Ladle.'

'But is *he*?' Fisk murmured thoughtfully.

'You can't be serious, Fisk,' Russell said. 'No man could survive a flooding like that. The water would have come in so fast . . . '

'I think we should take a look, don't you?'

Lights reflected on the still water of the flooded shaft. Bloated, mangled bodies floated amid the shattered timbers, but there wasn't one there with silver hair.

Fisk studied the water and then the platform, suddenly he pointed.

'There, on the platform, there's an area of dampness. Give me a lamp, someone.' He was handed a lamp and began to move away from the lip of the shaft towards the cavern wall. Finally he stopped and gestured to Russell. 'Come and see.'

Russell hurried over and Fisk pointed at the sandy floor by the cavern wall. There were several prints of a naked foot.

'I think I've just proved my point, Russell. Someone survived in the Ladle, climbed out on to the platform and then escaped. I'm betting it was Ben Travis. Now we have two men to hunt, no, three counting Jacob.' He smiled. 'I think tomorrow is going to be a rather interesting day.'

★ ★ ★

Wes cursed softly to himself as he pushed his way through the thick undergrowth. The trees around him grew thickly together causing him to make stumbling detours in the darkness. Occasionally the leafy canopy overhead thinned to enable moonlight to penetrate in silvery, smoky columns.

The island forest was never quiet and in the unnerving darkness leaves rustled as he disturbed some unseen creature. So far nothing had taken umbrage at his passing, deciding that attack was the best form of defence, and of that he was grateful.

Once he disturbed a bird, sending it screeching away into the darkness. He was looking for somewhere to rest for the night away from the rustling forest floor.

The invisible ground beneath his feet was sloping gently upwards and he just hoped it held no nasty surprises. He had already fallen down one bank he had not seen, ending up in a wet, muddy sinkhole. Apart from a few grazes and bruises, he had suffered no lasting damage, but . . . He decided not to dwell on the but.

Ahead, the darkness gave way to an uncertain grey light that made the trees ahead visible. He pushed on quicker and broke through the trees into a clearing frosted silver by the moon. Out of habit rather than necessity he dropped to one knee and scanned the area.

He had emerged on one side of a bowl-shaped, rocky depression some forty feet across, the moonlight giving the rocks a slick, icy look. A few stunted trees and clumps of scrub grew in scattered isolation in cracks between the rocks. At the bottom of the depression his eyes picked out the welcome gleam of a small pool, no more than ten feet across, that his throat hoped would be fresh water. The edges of the pool were hard mud, cracked and broken, showing that once it had been larger.

He scrambled down to the pool and a few minutes later was slaking his thirst with cool, fresh water. After a few minutes, he rose wearily to his feet. He was bone tired and could gladly have dropped where he stood, but caution prevailed. He cast around the moon-silvered landscape and his eyes settled on a rocky outcrop partway up a slope.

He climbed up to it on aching limbs and behind found a shallow hollow. What it lacked in comfort it made up for in protection. Not that he was looking for comfort this night; he felt he could sleep on a cactus if required. But sleep was the one thing that was denied him, for no sooner had he settled himself when he heard sounds from below coming from the area of the pool.

Something or someone big was crashing noisily through the under-growth on the far side of the tiny pool, then his heart jumped in his chest. He felt sure he heard a voice say 'Damn!' followed by more words that were less distinguishable. Sleep forgotten, he grabbed up a rifle and eased his head above the rocks.

Some of Fisk's men must have come after him and there could be more moving in. It was a thought that had not occurred to him, feeling safe in the idea that they would not start looking until daylight.

He muttered his own, 'Damn!' Waited a few minutes until the night had settled down once more, then he slipped out of the hollow and clambered down the slope, boots scraping as they slid on the rock, towards the pool.

Once on level ground, he moved

stealthily from one clump of scrub to the next. As he skirted the edge of the pool he heard sounds coming from a small copse of trees on the far side. Muffled voices again. Whoever was there was making no secret of his or their existence.

He circled the pool and crept into the trees from the rear. A twig snapped underfoot with the noise of a stick of dynamite going off; at least that was how it sounded to his straining ears.

He paused for a few minutes, then satisfied he had not been heard he inched through the trees towards the edge of the pool. The trees opened up to reveal a semi-circular clearing that led down to the water's edge.

Wes's nerves were humming as he paused on the edge of the clearing, eyes scanning the area quickly. The moon-light was hitting the trees from the side filling the clearing with dappled, silver light and deep shadow.

Gripping the rifle tighter, Wes peered intently into the shadows and his heart jumped; there was someone there, sitting against a tree trunk near to the water's edge and now he could hear breathing. It didn't make sense to him that if it was one of Fisk's men, one of the Gatherers, that the man should just be sitting down, apparently unconcerned.

A cold, uneasy feeling washed over him. He felt sure there had been more than one, so where was the other one?

The thought was still in his mind when he found out. The cold muzzle of a pistol was suddenly jammed hard against the back of his neck.

'Drop the rifle, *hombre*, less'n you want that fool head o' yours blown off.'

11

Wes let the rifle drop and raised his hands at the softly spoken, but authoritative, voice. He could scarcely believe his ears and prayed they were not letting him down.

'Think I'll pass on the offer. Makes it kinda' difficult for a fella to wear his hat. Ben, is that really you?' He swung round to face his attacker.

Ben Travis, the edge of a moonbeam slicing across his forehead making his silver hair glow, caught his breath.

'Wes? Tarnation!' he roared out happily. 'If'n you ain't a sight to make a grown man cry wi' joy.' He stepped forward, wrapped Wes in a bone-cracking bear-hug and lifted him off the ground.

'Dammit, Ben, I didn't come all this way to get my ribs bruk!' Wes protested breathlessly, and when Ben finally released him continued ruefully, 'First you threaten to blow my head off, next you're breaking my back. Anything else?'

'Fool head,' Ben corrected with a huge grin, then, 'What took you so long?'

'Had me a few chores to do,' Wes replied drily, his own face split in a wide grin. 'Who's your friend?'

'Don't rightly know, he can't speak. Bin beat pretty bad.'

'Jacob?' Wes moved across to the slumped figure.

'You know him?' Ben followed his partner.

'If'n it's who I think it is.' He hunkered down by the man. 'Jacob,' he said softly. The man stirred and lifted his head. 'It's me, Wes Hardiman. I visited wi' Bosun. Do you remember me?'

Jacob smiled wanly and nodded his head, placing a hand on Wes's arm. Wes capped his other hand over the other's weakly gripping fingers.

'He was whipped real bad,' Ben broke in softly. 'Fella wi' the handle o' The Bull. Well, he won't be whipping any more poor souls, less'n it's in Hell,' he ended darkly.

Wes nodded at his friend's words before addressing Jacob again.

'I'm real sorry 'bout Bosun, Jacob. Guess it was my fault coming to see him.' Jacob's fingers tightened on his arm and he shook his head. Reflected moonlight from the pool glinted on tears straining the other's cheeks.

Wes detached Jacob's hand from his arm and rose on creaking, popping knees. He turned to Ben.

'Got me a place up in the rocks just in case Fisk sends his men in early looking for me.'

'Sounds like you gotta story to tell,' Travis prompted.

'One you ain't gonna like,' Wes replied heavily. 'Let's get Jacob up to the rocks, it'll be safer there, an' I'll fill you in.'

'Well, I carried him this far, a few

more steps ain't gonna hurt.'

Jacob, on hearing the words, held his chin and waved a dismissive hand. Wes eyed Ben suspiciously and the big man smiled sheepishly.

'Jacob couldn't walk so well so I had to carry him from the mine. He was hurting real bad so I sorta persuaded him to go to sleep.'

'I get the picture,' Wes replied, and both men went across to the struggling Jacob and helped him to his feet.

It was a slow process, but Jacob made it to the rocks under his own steam and, once there, fell into a deep sleep leaving the other two to talk. Before that, Wes handed Ben a rifle, keeping a rifle and pistol for himself while Ben retained the derringer.

As the moon drifted across the star-scattered sky, Ben listened as Wes talked. The big man made no comment though his facial expression changed more than once.

' . . . So that's how it stands,' Wes concluded. 'Like I said, you ain't gonna like it 'cause come sun-up, Fisk is gonna send his men in looking for us, or rather me, an' you an' Jacob are gonna be in the firing line, so to speak.'

'Reckon when they found The Bull dead on the ground an' Jacob gone they figured there's gonna be more than one of us hiding out here,' Ben replied. 'So what's the plan?'

Wes shook his head. 'No plan, old friend, other than trying to stay alive, an' wi' the limited firepower we'uns have got, that ain't gonna be easy. Best we try and get some rest afore dawn. It might be a long time afore the next one.'

'Or pretty damn short,' Ben growled darkly.

★　★　★

The sun was already cresting the eastern ridge of the valley when Wes jerked awake and sat up. Ben and Jacob were already awake and shivering in the early morning chill. Wes felt the chill and he was fully dressed while Ben and Jacob were clad only in tattered pants. But at least Ben had the comfort of a pair of pinching boots, Jacob went bare-footed.

'Anything?' Wes joined Ben, peering along the long, narrow valley half submerged in a grey mist.

'Morning, pardner,' Ben greeted. 'Quiet as the grave out there.'

Wes smiled. 'Ain't exactly comforting words,' he remarked, before turning to Jacob. 'How are you today, Jacob?'

Jacob nodded and smiled, waving a hand. He showed more animation than yesterday and clambered to his feet unaided. Wes grimaced at the weals covering the man's body, arms and legs. Some had scabbed over, but movement caused them to ooze blood. Jacob must have been in some pain, but his face showed nothing.

They had no food, only water to sustain them and limited firepower. Ben's rifle had twelve shots, Wes's seven, with two in the pistol and two in the derringer; twenty-three shots in all. It was not much to wage a war on, let alone win it.

★   ★   ★

At the mine, Cabal Fisk completed the final preparations to flush Wes and the others from the valley. All mining operations had been shut down.

Within the great cavern, heavy iron gates had been padlocked across the mouths of the three remaining tunnels, locking the prisoners in. All the guards, along with the six remaining Gatherers; some thirty men in all, had assembled outside. All were armed and waited, grim-faced, for Fisk's orders.

Fisk smiled as he sauntered over to Russell. 'A fine day, don't you think, Sheriff?' he called lightly. 'And one that has all the makings of getting better.'

'Get on with it, Fisk. This place is starting to give me the creeps.' Russell stood with coat collar turned up against the early morning chill; hands thrust in pockets. He peered moodily about before finally settling his sour gaze on the ever smiling Fisk.

'Patience, Sheriff. We will be away at the next turn of the tide.' He turned to the nearest man. 'Bring the dogs!' The man nodded and hurried away.

Russell raised an eyebrow. 'Them goddam vicious brutes? I thought you wanted Hardiman alive?'

'I had a change of heart overnight. I let my more humane side rule my head.'

'You call getting ripped to pieces by them critters humane?'

'Not for Hardiman and whoever else is out there. I was thinking more of the dogs: they haven't eaten for some time,' Fisk explained, and burst into laughter.

There were four dogs in all: huge, black, snarling, cross-bred brutes, straining on rope leads. Each dog had its own handler to whom it responded and each handler had tried to make his animal the most vicious.

The guards moved rapidly aside as

the dogs were brought in, the animals making sudden growling, snapping lunges at the nearest man.

The dogs were taken to the head of the valley. Fisk gave the order and the animals were released. Barking and snarling, they disappeared into the undergrowth and the handlers plunged after them. Finally the guards led by the Gatherers followed, but Fisk kept two men back whom he sent to *The Hawk* with a message to Captain Hollister.

Fisk lit a cigar and sighed contentedly as he cast Sheriff Russell a glance.

'Yes, I feel this day has greatness to it.'

★ ★ ★

In the valley the three were on the move. They had decided to take the offensive; move on the enemy rather than wait for the enemy to find them.

'Damn boots,' Ben groaned, wincing as he limped, his handsome face running a gamut of expressions.

'You should have taken them off while we rested,' Wes said.

'If'n I'd'a done that I reckon I wouldn't have got them on agin,' he grumbled.

A few feet in front, Jacob, unconcerned that he was bare-footed, halted suddenly and signalled to the others before cupping a hand to an ear.

'What is it, Jacob?' Wes asked softly, then he heard it and threw Ben a glance.

'They've put the dogs on us,' Ben breathed, as his ears caught the distant barking. 'From what I heard 'bout them hounds, they love the taste o' human flesh an' then some.'

They had travelled about halfway along the valley bottom hidden beneath the canopy of trees, safe from searching eyes, but not from dogs.

'We need higher, more open, ground,' Wes said.

'I'm wi' you, pardner,' Ben agreed, his feet forgotten as they prepared to meet a new enemy.

* ★ *

Sheriff Russell watched with narrowed eyes as Captain Hollister of *The Hawk* joined Fisk. He had brought some thirty crewmen, laden with barrels of gunpowder, that they carried into the mine and stacked in a pile.

'What's going on, Fisk?' he demanded.

'It's time to finish up here. With the Devil's Ladle gone the mine is useless.'

'What about the men inside?'

'What about them?' Fisk countered.

Russell ran a hand across his lips; he suddenly had a bad taste in his mouth.

'The tide will be turning in an hour. Is that not right, Captain?' Fisk flashed the captain a glance and at the man's nod, returned his gaze to Russell. 'That should give us plenty of time to complete our task here and be on our way.'

'Will they be finished in the valley and back here by then?'

Fisk shook his head sadly; his eyes had grown cold, almost hostile.

'Sheriff, you are starting to worry me,' he said softly, and a cold chill touched Russell's heart. 'The men in the mine are expendable; the men in the valley are expendable. Are you expendable, Sheriff?'

For the first time, Sheriff Russell felt a pang of fear lance through him. Unconsciously his hand dropped to the butt of his pistol. If Fisk saw the move he ignored it.

'*The Hawk* is loaded with gold ore. You will be a rich man, Sheriff, and I will be even richer.' He smiled at the thought. 'I intend leaving Galveston, moving east, but first we must clear up here. Don't you agree?'

Russell nodded dumbly, finding it difficult to speak.

'Yes, sure. Guess I wasn't thinking straight,' he finally mumbled, and Fisk smiled and nodded, reached across and patted his arm.

'But you are now. That's the spirit.'

★ ★ ★

They didn't see the dog immediately, but they heard it; a low, rumbling snarl that came from above them.

The three had moved to one side of the valley. Here the trees were thinner and the ground sloping, scree piles held together with clumps of thorny brush. It climbed away in a series of step-like ledges before rising sheer to the sky in a towering cliff face. It was from the lowest of the ledges, a few feet above their heads, that the sound came.

Three heads snapped up together and eyes focused on the black, pug-nosed animal. Its lips were pulled back revealing sharp white teeth in red gums. Saliva drooled from its mouth, dropping in long, silver strings, while eyes, black, shining pearls set in black velvet fur regarded them.

They only had a brief glimpse. As both Wes and Ben swung their rifles up the animal was gone, leaping from the ledge on to Jacob.

Jacob went down and man and animal rolled down a short slope together. Jacob had managed to get a hand around the animal's throat, keeping the snapping, snarling mouth from tearing out his own throat.

Jacob wrapped his other arm over the dog's back, hugging it to his body to stop the raking claws from gouging his flesh. He gripped the throat tightly and pushed the drooling head up.

Wes and Ben had charged down the slope, yelling and shouting in an effort to put the animal off, but they dared not use their weapons. Man and beast were so tightly entangled that no clear shot was available. All they could do was stand by helplessly and watch, waiting for an opportunity.

Sweat appeared on Jacob's face. Slowly his arm began to straighten forcing the slavering mouth away from his face, forcing the dog's head back until its muzzle pointed at the sky.

There was a snap and crunch of bone as the dog's neck broke and the animal went limp. Jacob threw the dead animal to one side. The big man's heaving chest was covered in blood where the dog's claws had torn the flesh.

As Ben darted forward to help Jacob up, Wes heard a sound from above and whirled, angling the rifle up for a hip shot. A man appeared above — it was the dog's handler — and Wes fired. The man cried out as the bullet ploughed into his chest, slamming him back against the rock wall. He bounced forward and then toppled from the ledge, rolling down the slope until a clump of scrub stopped him.

The second dog appeared from the trees at the bottom of the slope and flew towards Ben and Jacob. Wes calmly levered a bullet into the breech, raised the rifle to his shoulder, fired, levered and fired a second time. Both bullets hit the animal, causing crimson sprays to erupt from its fur. The second bullet spun the animal on its back and it lay still.

It sickened Wes to kill the dog; he remembered his own dog when he was a boy. But those dogs had been trained to kill and he had been trained to stay alive.

'How's Jacob?' he called out anxiously.

'Leakin' a tad, but OK,' Ben replied with grim humour.

'The shots will have alerted anyone looking to our position. Things are gonna get a mite hairy from now on in,' Wes said grimly.

★ ★ ★

Fisk watched intently as barrels of kerosene, stored at the mine for use in the lamps, were rolled to a point where the ground fell away steeply into the valley below, disappearing into a thicket of dense scrub and brush. Fisk ordered the barrels to be breeched and the contents emptied down the slope. Nearly thirty barrels were emptied in this fashion, filling the warm air with strong fumes.

'Is that gonna be enough?' Russell questioned.

'This time of the year the valley tends to be at its driest. Should burn pretty good.'

'What if a passing ship sees the smoke?'

'It'll keep on passing. No captain's gonna risk his boat to look at a fire on a deserted island; especially this one. Stop worrying, Sheriff.'

'There could be survivors. What then?'

'Then they'll die of starvation. There's no way off this island. There's no food, no water, no hope.' Fisk hunkered down, pulled a lucifer from his pocket, struck it on a rock and applied the flame to the kerosene-soaked slope. A tiny blue flame shot up and began to descend rapidly into the valley.

It took about five minutes before the first columns of smoke began to spiral into the air accompanied by the crackle of burning vegetation. In the far distance, the sporadic gunfire of an unseen battle reached their ears.

'It appears that hunters and hunted have finally met up with each other,' Fisk said. 'Come, Sheriff, just one more task and we can leave this island.' He walked across to where a black trail of gunpowder led into the mine. He handed Russell a lucifer and, smiling said, 'Be my guest, Sheriff.' He stepped back as Russell crouched, scraped the lucifer into life and applied it to the gunpowder.

Tiny sparks leaped and danced as the gunpowder ignited and the sheriff rose to his feet. He heard the gunshot, very close and loud, and at almost the same instant felt a hard *punch* in the middle of his back. He was still looking downwards when the bullet exited out through his stomach in a ghastly spray of blood and fragments of gut.

Russell spun in shock, his hands clasping his stomach. He saw Cabal Fisk, five yards away, a smoking gun in his fist, a smile on his face.

'You became expendable when you started to worry, Boyd, and a worried man means trouble. Can't keep his mouth shut. This way you stop worrying and I don't get any trouble.'

Russell sank to his knees, blood pumping out between his fingers.

'Bastard!' The word came from Russell's mouth wrapped in a torrent of blood.

'I probably am,' Fisk agreed. 'I probably am.' He turned away as Russell toppled forward and lay still. 'Come, Captain, we have a tide to catch.'

★   ★   ★

The three were pinned down behind some rocks. Bullets flew from the trees, ricocheting from the rocks with an angry whine. Crouched in the trees, the black-clad Clay Rutters signalled for a ceasefire.

'You in the rocks. Got more'n twenty men here. Throw your guns down an' come out or the dogs come in.' To add weight to his words the two remaining dogs barked and snarled, straining at the ropes in their handlers' hands.

Wes and Ben eyed each other.

'Reckon I'll pass on that offer,' Ben called out.

Rutters scowled and glared across at the handlers.

'When I say so, let them hell-hounds loose. Rest o' you boys, we follow them critters an' what they don't finish, we do.' He eyed the handlers again. 'Let 'em go!'

Wes and Ben along with Jacob had moved as far back from the rocks as they could and now sat with their backs to a wall, rifles slanted up from the hip.

'Them dogs'll have to come over the rocks. They'll be moving real fast. Reckon we'll have one shot each. If'n one comes over first, I'll take it. Both together, you take the one on the right.' Wes had rattled out the words, now they waited.

'If'n I was them boys I'd follow them hounds up,' Ben whispered and Wes nodded.

They heard the scrape of claws,

low-throated snarling and like black shadows from a nightmare the two dogs appeared on the top of the rocks. Both men fired together. Ben's bullet caught his animal full in the chest throwing it backwards the way it had come. Wes's bullet caught his animal square between the eyes and it fell at his feet, head shattered.

By that time Ben was up. The attacking men were already out of the trees and charging towards the rocks as Ben started firing, joined a second later by Wes.

Caught out in the open and under a withering hail of fire eight went down. The remainder scattered, returning to the cover of the trees.

'That evened it up a little,' Ben cried.

'Not enough though,' Wes returned.

'It'll have to do. I'm clean outa shells.' Ben lay the empty rifle down with a rueful smile.

Wes hefted his pistol after tossing his rifle aside.

'Two shots left.'

'Same here.' Ben held up the derringer. 'Gotta be real close to make any difference wi' this.' He sniffed. 'Do you smell smoke?'

'An' something else. Kerosene.'

There was a commotion from the men in the trees. Wes and Ben risked a peep over the rocks. Black smoke was drifting through the trees and the men were staggering out, coughing and spluttering, heedless of any bullets that might come their way.

Above the trees, a thick pall of smoke was hanging. A sudden, distant explosion rent the air. It came from the area of the mine.

'I ain't too sure what's going on, but I got a bad feeling,' Wes said.

As the rumble of the explosion faded away, the crackle and snap of burning twigs filled their ears. The cries from the men were more urgent now. They were running from the trees, running towards the rocks when a sheet of flame roared out of the trees and engulfed them.

12

Before their horrified eyes, the running men became engulfed in a wall of searing flame that surged forward, then shrank back to the edge of the trees. In its wake it left the slope littered with black, smouldering bodies.

Clouds of choking smoke drifted away from the blazing tree-line towards them.

'Back to the pool!' Wes shouted.

The three began to run, their aches and pains forgotten. Behind them, the flames fanned by a light, east/west breeze funnelling down the valley from the mine, chased them.

The hungry, crackling flames were close on their heels when the three reached the pool and plunged in, the shallow water cooling their sweating bodies.

They stayed in the centre of the pool

for the next hour as the fire circled around them. Finally, as the flames died back and they climbed from the water, an amazing yet sad sight met their eyes.

They could see right down the valley now; a valley of black, charred posts, all that was left of the trees, rising from the hot, smouldering ashes. All was overlaid by a pall of grey smoke that hung like an autumn mist in the air. A vista of black and grey destruction. It was a humbling sight.

They said very little as they made their way to the end of the valley and clambered out of the eye-watering greyness to the clear air around the mine, or what remained of it. The explosion had brought half the cliff down, destroying the entrance and burying it beneath tons of rock.

The body of Sheriff Russell lay where it had fallen.

'Guess they had a falling out,' Wes surmised; there was no compassion in his voice.

Ben's gaze drifted to the destroyed

mine and his eyes grew hard, hands balling into fists at his sides.

'I kinda doubt Fisk released the prisoners afore he destroyed the evidence.' He turned to Wes. 'I want that *hombre*, real bad, Wes.'

'Join the queue, pard,' Wes replied coldly. Jacob stepped forward catching hold of Wes's arm. His big, round eyes flashed on both of them and he pointed at himself. 'Guess you want him too, eh, Jacob?' The big man nodded and Wes looked across at Ben. 'Looks like we both stand in line.'

'Could be a long wait,' Ben said gloomily. 'How do we get off this damn island?'

★ ★ ★

The answer to the question came an hour later, and while Wes and Ben stared at it appalled, Jacob was smiling.

The three had trekked down to the now empty cove. The tide had receded to reveal a narrow ribbon of sand that allowed access to the next cove and it was here they found it. The cove was a glory-hole of washed-up flotsam and jetsam from the sea. Amid the tangle of seaweed, broken timbers, rigging and ropes lay the boat.

It was small, probably a lifeboat from one of the many wrecks that littered the rocks, partially buried in sea debris and half full of water.

'Ain't too sure what you're smiling for, Jacob,' Ben said sourly, but Jacob continued to smile. He pointed to the sea and made rowing motions with his hands.

'I think he has the notion to row us out of here in that,' Wes said.

'I was afraid that's what he meant,' Ben replied, staring out to sea at the distant reef of rocks; hearing the waves crash against them; seeing the fantails of white spray leap high into the air. 'Is that thing gonna float?' He looked back unhappily at the others.

'Only one way to find out,' Wes replied.

It took them almost another hour to empty the boat of water, dig it from the sand and drag it down to the foreshore. Jacob examined it and nodded enthusiastically at the two.

'Damn!' Ben muttered under his breath and Wes laughed.

'We got two choices here, Ben: we stay an' die o' thirst an' starvation or take our chances at sea.'

'An' die quicker,' Ben grumbled. 'There's some darn big catfish out there wi' teeth you ain't ever seen the likes o' afore.' He shivered as he remembered the shark in the flooded shaft.

It was midday when they put to sea. Jacob had found a pair of oars amid the flotsam and jetsam of the cove and with smooth, even strokes pulled them away from the shore.

The boat possessed a broken tiller, but there was enough of it remaining for a man to work the rudder. Wes took control of it while Ben, sitting in the bottom of the boat between Wes's knees, gripped the sides with both hands. Wes soon got used to steering the small craft as they headed out across the bay towards the waiting rocks.

The oars creaked in brass rowlocks that rattled loosely in their fittings. It was smooth going for the first few minutes, but as they neared the inner edge of the reef, the water became choppy. Spray from the waves pounding the rocks began to fall like fine rain over them and soon all three were soaked. Rowing opened up the fresher cuts and gouges on Jacob's chest, mingling with the spray to form a gruesome, red shroud that soaked into the tattered remnants of his once white pants. Wes guessed the man was in pain, but it did not affect his rowing.

The tiny craft sped between rocks that now towered above them and beneath arches of dazzling, white spray. Wes tightened his grip on the tiller, pushing and pulling it, steering the craft away from the foaming rocks.

They forged ever deeper into a white,

drenching world of ceaseless thunder that pounded like some terrible drum in their ears. The boat dipped into troughs and surged up on swells. Leaving the water at times only to smack down seconds later with a bone-jarring crash.

For Ben, with nothing to do but sit there and hold on, it was an unbelievable nightmare. Water slopped over the sides of the boat, surging back and forth as it dipped and rose.

Jacob was losing control of the oars in the growing turmoil of the water. Ben crawled forward and grabbed an oar, seating himself next to the man. Jacob flashed him a grateful look.

They could not see back to the island or ahead to the open sea. The spray was like a thick fog, the rocks black, threatening, monsters that suddenly appeared from it. The spray lashed their eyes, half blinding them.

The boat scraped a rock and then disaster struck. They dropped into a trough and the rudder shattered as it hit a rock. The tiller went light in Wes's grip and he almost went over the side. Jacob and Ben fought to control the boat with the oars then Jacob's oar snapped in half as the boat was pushed sideways against a wall of rock. The section of gunwale holding the rowlock splintered and came away. Ben dug in his oar and held on, slewing the boat away from the rocks.

The keel of the boat hit rock. Wood splintered as the hull was breeched. Wes lurched forward onto his knees, tearing the shirt from his back, balling it and ramming it into the hole. It seemed a pointless gesture, for now, with virtually no control over the boat, there was little chance of them surviving the chilling, reef of rocks. Soon they would become more victims of the Isla de la Muerte.

Ben's oar snapped as it caught on a hidden snag in the foaming, angry water. He flew over backwards cracking his head on the floor of the boat that, with no controlling hand, spun and twisted in the wrathful grip of the sea.

Water poured in over the gunwales. Grimly, the three held on as the boat crunched against the razor-sharp rocks, first one side and then the other. Waves lifted the little boat and threw it forward into a roaring, frothing fan of rising spray and they waited for the moment of impact that would shatter the frail craft into a thousand pieces, their bodies along with it.

Blue sky seared their half-blind eyes and sunlight exploded warm and welcoming over their bodies as the boat shot through the wall of spray and out into the open. It hit the water and settled sluggishly on the calm sea beyond, subsiding currents pushing it away from the deadly rocks. They sat up, disbelief in their salt-reddened eyes. They had made it through the reef!

Jubilation lifted them high for a few moments, Wes and Ben shouting idiotically to the skies, Jacob grinning widely. They hugged each other — almost capsizing the small, battered boat in their joy. Then reality brought them back to earth: the boat, already half full of water, was slowly sinking. Galvanized into action they began scooping the water out using cupped hands.

'It's that damn hole in the bottom,' Wes shouted. The shirt plug was still in place, but water was soaking through it. Ben, in a moment of inspiration, began to tug off his boots and finally had to get Wes to help him.

'Goddam boots!' He yelled as eventually, reluctantly, one came off in Wes's hands. 'Knew they'd come in useful one day.' He took the boot from Wes, wound the high side around the foot forming a tight, leather tube and then rammed it into the hole pushing the shirt plug out. It proved to be a tight, almost waterproof fit.

Wes wrestled the other boot off and Ben let out a sigh of relief, wriggling his cramped toes.

'If'n that ain't just dandy,' Ben sang out. 'Gotta use for this'n too,' he said taking it from Wes and then proceeding to use it as a scoop.

Wes chuckled his appreciation at Ben's idea then pulled his own boots off, passed one to Jacob and they all began bailing. It took twenty exhausting minutes until just two inches of water remained and they collapsed tiredly into the bottom of the boat.

Wes sat up after a few minutes and stared around. Except for the island receding behind them and to the west, no land showed in any other direction and they appeared to be drifting east.

'Which way's home, Jacob?'

Jacob pointed to the north. With a dropping heart, Wes knew that without a means of steering the boat they were at the whim of the currents. Jacob began to use a hand as a paddle, turning the boat until its prow pointed north. The other two joined in and slowly but surely they began to head north. It was a tiring business. Later, Wes had another idea. Slipping over the side he gripped the rear of the boat and used his feet to propel it forward. After twenty minutes he had to be pulled aboard, exhausted, and Ben took over.

Ben lasted for half an hour before he, too, was pulled out. They had made some headway, but now they were drifting east again. Throats dry and raw, bodies exhausted, sick headaches beating at their temples from the remorseless sun, they could do nothing but sprawl in the bottom of the boat to wait and hope that some passing ship would spot them. They had exchanged one kind of hell for another.

The sun was already dipping towards the west when Wes felt his arm being shaken. He must have fallen asleep. He stared blearily up at Jacob.

'What is it?' Wes croaked, his voice a hoarse whisper.

Jacob continued to shake him, pointing out to sea at the same time. Wes shook his aching head and roused himself to peer in the direction Jacob was pointing. Instantly, his own aches and pains forgotten, he roused Ben.

'There's a ship out there, Ben,' he

rasped. 'Rouse yoursel', pard, this may be our only chance.'

They all climbed carefully to their feet and began waving their arms. At first it seemed that the distant ship, a single-sailed sloop, would continue on its way oblivious to them, then slowly it turned and headed towards them.

'It's seen us!' Ben yelled, or as much as he could yell.

Fifteen minutes later, Wes's eyes lit up.

'It's *The Colleen*, Sean Flynne's boat,' he croaked.

Ten minutes later, willing hands hauled them aboard *The Colleen* to the grinning delight of Sean Flynne. Even better for the boys; Siobhan had accompanied her brother.

'When *The Hawk* returned and you never appeared, Wes, we decided to come looking for you,' Sean explained later.

'I'm obliged you did,' Wes replied.

'Reckon we was ready to float clear to Chinee,' Ben announced grandly.

''Tis glad we are to have saved the poor Chinese people the pitiful sight o' you,' Siobhan cried, eyeing Ben, a smile of happiness on her face.

'So what happened out there?' Sean wanted to know, and between them the two unfolded their stories.

Darkness had long since fallen by the time *The Colleen* docked at Galveston. Wes wanted their presence kept secret for the time-being so Siobhan led them into the tavern via a rear door and into a quiet back-room.

The two had recovered quickly from their ordeal, but Jacob was a cause for concern. He had lost a lot of blood on top of everything else that had happened, and they had to almost carry him from the boat. Siobhan dressed his wounds and they left him sleeping in an upstairs bedroom.

There was a bath-house out back of the tavern, and while Wes and Ben bathed, Siobhan prepared food for them. It was almost midnight by the time the two had eaten, washed the food down with three mugs of coffee and chased the coffee with a couple of whiskies. Both were almost out on their feet and fell into their beds gratefully, asleep in seconds.

It was mid-morning before they woke and the appetizing smell of bacon led them to the kitchen. To their surprise and delight, Jacob was already up and wolfing down a large breakfast. He smiled brightly and waved them a greeting.

Sean came in as they were finishing their breakfast; his face was grim.

'It looks like Fisk is preparing to leave,' he announced without preamble. 'There's a lot of activity at his house. What do we do?'

'Stop him,' Wes said grimly. He looked up at Sean. 'We'll need a dozen men, more if possible, wi' guns an' who ain't afraid to use 'em.'

'You'll have them,' Sean promised.

'We'll also need some means of getting to Fisk's quickly.'

'I'll get some wagons. Anything else?'

'Dynamite,' Ben chipped in. 'Ain't nothing better to make a man keep his head down and stay put than some damn fool tossing dynamite about.'

'You shall have it,' Sean replied.

'One other thing,' Wes threw in casually. 'Would you happen to know where Bryce is?'

'Him and his men are at Fisk's.'

Wes nodded to himself. 'Now that's real fine,' he mused. 'When can we be ready to move?'

'Thirty minutes.'

Sean was true to his word. Thirty minutes later, two wagons rolled out of town carrying fifteen grim-faced men plus Wes, Ben and Sean. The two were back in their normal clothes now. Ben in buckskin with his moccasin boots; Wes, in denim range clothes, a black, leather vest over a blue shirt. His spare gun was strapped to his waist. Once clear of the town, the drivers whipped up their teams to a gallop.

Bryce was with Fisk in an upstairs study when there was a commotion from outside. A rattle of gunshots; men shouting. Bryce crossed the room quickly and stepped outside on to the veranda, drawing his gun.

Three of his men lay dead on the ground while the others had retreated to any cover they could find, returning fire with a group of men who were attacking the house. His eyes picked out two familiar figures with the attackers and he sucked in breath hurriedly before moving back into the study, almost colliding with Fisk.

'What's going on?' Fisk demanded.

'I thought you said them two fellas, Hardiman and Travis, were dead?'

'They are. They died on the island.'

'Then it must be their twin brothers out there.'

Fisk darted out onto the veranda and when he came back into the room his face was white.

'It's not possible. The dogs, the fire. Even if they survived them, there is no way off the island.' There was an almost supernatural fear in his eyes.

'Mebbe you should tell 'em that 'cause they don't seem to know,' Bryce said casually.

'Fisk! Cabal Fisk. It's Wes Hardiman. Give yourself up. There ain't no way out.' Wes's voice floated up to them. 'We have captured *The Hawk* and Captain Hollister.'

An explosion rocked the house.

'Dammit! They're using dynamite,' Bryce said.

'My friend here ain't too happy with what you did to the mine an' all those people you left in it,' Wes's voice came again. 'Come out, Fisk, afore he does the same to you.'

Fisk rounded on Bryce. 'I paid you to protect me, Bryce; so protect!' he snarled.

★　★　★

Fisk's house was a large, southern-style mansion. White-walled with three storeys, each circled by a veranda. It was like a giant wedding cake; the supporting pillars and ornate veranda railings blue. The grounds surrounding the house were beautifully laid out, their borders magnificent drifts of colour; lawns like soft, green velvet, now defaced by a number of dead bodies.

A number of stone statues were dotted about the grounds before the house and it was behind these that Sean's men, along with Wes and Ben, hid. They watched the wide, pillared entrance, its once ornate double doors shattered, blown inwards, and strewn about the big reception hall beyond. Smoke drifted from the entrance and Wes tensed: a figure moved in the smoke.

Bryce stepped out through the ruined entrance.

'Where's Fisk?' Wes called.

'Ain't Fisk you gotta be worried 'bout, Cowboy. Reckon you an' me have got some unfinished business, if'n you think you can?' There was a contemptuous note in his voice that stung Wes.

Wes stepped out from behind the statue.

'That's what I'm here for, Bryce.' Wes stalked forward as he spoke, closing the distance between them.

Bryce smiled. His hands hung loosely at his sides, right hand within an inch of his holstered Colt. They locked eyes. Bryce's face was calm, emotionless, except for the infuriating smile.

Most gunslingers like to get it over quick. If a man had too much time to think then he could start to doubt himself and that could slow his draw. But Bryce did not seem to be in a hurry. He was playing a game of nerves, trying to unsettle his opponent; but it was a game two could play.

Slowly, unhurriedly, Wes folded his arms across his chest, keeping his stare locked on Bryce. It was the ultimate move in the game. A show of arrogant disregard of his opponent; a move that could easily get him killed.

'Whenever you're ready, Bryce. If ever you are?' The final taunt. His heart was beating rapidly against his folded arms.

Unease sprang into Bryce's eyes. A tic fluttered in the corner of one eye. He made his move. His draw was liquid smooth; every move honed to perfection.

It was difficult to say who fired first for both pistols roared in unison. Wes turned sideways as he drew and fired, presenting a smaller target. Bryce remained facing him. Wes heard Bryce's bullet pass by, very close by. His bullet caught Bryce in the throat, blowing the back of his neck away as it exited.

Wes was trembling as he reholstered his gun.

'You trying to get yoursel' killed?' Ben yelled angrily. 'What was that darn fool arm-folding play?'

'Something I ain't gonna try again,' Wes replied, and Ben suddenly smiled.

'Sure was pretty though. Best give Fisk a reminder.' Ben lit the fuse on a second stick of dynamite and lobbed it through the shattered doorway. A few seconds later, a section of the wall to the left of the doorway blew outwards.

Smoke billowed out as glass smashed and flames licked out through the shattered wall.

'Come out now, Fisk, or you'll burn in life like you're gonna burn in Hell,' Ben roared out.

'We got him!' Two men hurried around the corner of the house with Fisk between them. 'He was trying to creep out the back.'

'That figures,' Wes replied. 'End of the line for you, Cabal. Reckon you'll hang for this.'

'Hang for what, Mr Hardiman? You appear to have got rid of any evidence,' — he nodded at the dead Bryce — 'you might have had against me.' The fire in the house was beginning to take hold now. Flames were leaping from the second-storey windows while smoke billowed from those above. He cast an amused eye at the burning house before looking back at Wes. 'And there goes any written evidence. We think along the same lines, Wes. Fire is the best cleanser of all. I don't think you will be able to prove anything against me that I can't nudge in the direction of those less fortunate than myself. Poor Bryce.'

'We still have Captain Hollister,' Wes pointed out.

'Take me in, Wes. I'm sure my lawyers will sort out this silly mistake,' Fisk smiled. Behind him the second-storey veranda collapsed with a crash.

Jacob moved purposefully towards Fisk. Fisk saw him coming and alarm showed in his face. He backed up a step or two. Jacob kept on coming. Then, before the others realized what was happening, Fisk produced a Remington .38 from a pocket and aimed it at the approaching man.

'Stop, damn you,' he cried, and at close range fired twice into the man's chest.

Jacob's step faltered for a second before he closed on Fisk and wrapped his big arms around the other.

Wes and Ben moved forward. Fisk was struggling in Jacob's iron grip. In a tremendous bearhug Jacob was slowly, but surely, squeezing the man to death.

Above the crackle of flames, Wes heard the ominous snapping of bones. Fisk cried out, his face a mask of agony as his breaking ribs were pushed into his lungs.

'Jacob, let him go. Let the law deal wi' him,' Wes cried.

The silent Jacob stared at the flames. He remembered the cries of Bosun as the old man perished in the burning cabin, and tears sprang into his eyes.

No one was ready for what happened next. In a stumbling lurch, and still gripping Fisk in his arms, Jacob headed for the burning house. No one knew until the last minute what he was going to do, but by then it was too late.

Blood was running from Cabal Fisk's lips, but he was still alive as Jacob carried him into the burning inferno of the house.

★ ★ ★

Two days later, Wes and Ben climbed aboard the train that would take them back to Tucson. Wes had retrieved his hat and gunbelt from *The Hawk* and they had said their goodbyes to Siobhan and Sean Flynne.

'Why do you think Jacob did what he did?' Ben asked gloomily.

'He knew Fisk was responsible for Bosun's death and he could see that Fisk was going to get away wi' it, so he made sure no clever lawyers would set Fisk free.'

'But taking his own life?'

'He already had two bullets in him. I reckon it was Jacob's final tribute to Bosun. Guess he really loved that old man.'

The train jerked into movement.

'Can't say I won't be sorry if'n I never lay eyes on the sea again,' Ben spoke up after a few minutes. 'Think I'll stick to sand an' cactus, an folks who call me mister instead o' shipmate.'

'Not to mention the 'catfish',' Wes said grinning wickedly.

'Damn!' Ben shivered. 'Sure wish you hadn't.'

THE END